THE HEIST

PHA PRESS

THE HEIST

...dogs bark the loudest on quiet nights

A Novel
by
PETE HANNIFORD

PHA PRESS

For more information address:
Email: petehanniford@phapress.co.uk

Printed in the United States of America

ISBN 13: 978-976-95644-1-1

For my children

Table of Contents

PART III: The Aftermath 154

⚔ Prologue ⚔

NIGHTMARES

Dogs bark the loudest on quiet nights. Vic could hear the grunts and slurs of the drunken brewers.

'How on earth are we going to move fifty barrels on a night like this?' said Vic to Randy, his sidekick.

'We need a mule,' stated Randy with an annoying laugh.

Vic needed at least forty barrels to balance his books. The other ten would be for paying off Randy and his two greedy stragglers. It was time to move in for the kill. Vic covered his face with a ski mask, while the carefree Randy and his pals went in with their uncovered faces. The entry was easy. The drunken brewers were too knackered to know what was going on under their noses. It would take the guys at least three hours to move fifty barrels; It was after forty when the sound of sirens came pouring in the direction of the Great Whisky Heist.

'This is the perfect night. How on earth did the Old Bill know about this?' a puzzled Vic asked himself.

Without wasting a minute the cops announced, 'It's over Vic, come out with your hands on your head!'

The surprised Vic did not know what to do. He wished he could turn into an ant and crawl through a hole. He looked around and his accomplices were nowhere in sight. He had no choice but to give up, and so he did.

Vic was awakened by the feeling of cold steel on his wrist. He leapt up like a man that had been saved from drowning. To his relief the steel belonged to Francis, his huge overfed pit bull.

'It was all a dream,' he thought to himself.

But, the reality remains, he needs fifty barrels of brew to balance his books and pay off his creditors or he will be out of business.

✕ PART I ✕

THE PREAMBLE

≍ 1 ≍

THE REFUGE

Early nineties London, the demand for hard liquor was high. People needed something to warm up the body during those cold winters, and the dockworkers needed something or somewhere to take their minds off their misery.

Vic Montgomery was the proud, but sorry owner of a broken-down pub called 'Vic's'. His patrons could hardly afford to buy a pint of beer. He had to give out complimentary drinks just to keep them coming back.

Fifty years ago Vic's known then as The Refuge, was a prestigious and very profitable pub established just before World War Two. It was owned by a wealthy tradesman named Patrick Carlisle. The Refuge was more sophisticated. The outside was covered with beautiful red bricks, and the inside was coated with the finest mahogany. Crystal chandeliers brightened the ceiling with the sparkle of red, blue and green lights. As the name suggested, the pub was mostly frequented by lawyers, doctors and politicians, who needed an escape from their busy lives and annoying wives.

After the war when everything returned to normal and the working class society was rejuvenated, Patrick Carlisle would normally put on various events at The Refuge, and the pub hosted some of the biggest dart tournaments in London. On one memorable night, one eyed Jerry McCain needed a bull's-eye to win the one thousand pounds grand prize; however his vision was distorted by second place Robert 'Precision Bob' Nelson.

Just as one-eyed Jerry McCain was about to make the victory throw, Precision Bob shouted 'Look Jerry! I found your eye!'

Jerry was so happy with the news of his missing eye that he completely missed the dartboard and the dart ended up in the behind of Big Jake Malloy who screamed in agony. Big Jake was in so much pain that he gobbled down a bottle of whisky without stopping for air. By the time he'd finished, Big Jake was furious and his face was burning red as he dashed across the room toward one-eyed Jerry McCain. When Jerry saw the four hundred pound Jake coming, he rushed behind the bar to get some cover. Before Jake reached the counter he started throwing beer mugs and furniture towards the bar. When he arrived at the counter he tried to get hold of one-eyed Jerry, but was unable to grab him because Jerry was moving from side to side (as if he was dancing the tango with Jake). Big Jake then decided to leap over the counter but his belly blocked the effort and a section collapsed. One-eyed Jerry decided that he had to cool down Big Jake's rage, so he leapt up from behind the bar with the faucet; and started to spray Big Jake with beer, emptying the entire canister on him. After the beer shower was over, Big Jake looked like Santa Claus donning a fully grown beard. He fell over on his back gasping for air; he could not move a muscle and there his pursuit of one-eyed Jerry came to an abrupt halt. Big Jake was breathing hard, he tried to talk but it seemed as though his tongue was half-way down his throat. All he could do was gesture with his hands; showing clearly what he intended to say if his larynx was in working order.

One-eyed Jerry grinned cheekily and then went to the bar to grab a bottle of whisky and two glasses. He went over to Big Jake whose tongue was by this time dislodged from his throat. Both men downed the bottle, still arguing about who the victor was, although one-eyed Jerry was more concerned about the one thousand pounds dart prize (which was indeed a tidy sum). He had always dominated the dart-board at the 'Refuge' and it was where he earned his living and he was very successful when Precision Bob was not in the game. The one thousand pounds was the biggest prize ever, and was like a golden egg to Jerry. He taunted the other punters for weeks before the tournament. He would walk in and inhale deeply, savoring the delicious smell of ten and twenty pound notes.

With all this going on, Patrick Carlisle did not attempt to put a stop to the fiasco because it was free entertainment and the patrons seemed to enjoy the show. After it was all over (or so he thought), Patrick Carlisle announced that the one thousand pounds grand prize money would be used to repair the damage. One-eyed Jerry was not pleased with the announcement and murmured something about being on top of the leader board and that Robert 'Precision Bob' Nelson was to blame for the missed throw. He started to shout his lungs out and headed in the direction of Precision Bob. Precision Bob saw that Jerry was senselessly drunk and knew that he had to make a fast exit, because a drunken Jerry was like a rabid dog using its canines as a weapon. Jerry leapt after Precision Bob, but Precision Bob was too fast and, he rapidly removed his body from the oncoming impact. Jerry's onslaught ended in the direction of the games slot machine. The impact did not seem to affect Jerry, even though blood was leaking down his forehead. He picked himself up scanning the room for a new victim; as the only satisfaction he could salvage from the night would be hurting somebody. Looking for an easy target, his eyes caught and remained focused on Patrick Carlisle. He spotted a half-empty bottle of whisky on a table about half-way between himself and Carlisle. He walked over slowly, gobbled down a fraction of what was in the bottle, looked at Carlisle again, then shouted, 'You cheating bastard!' and threw the bottle. It ended up at the back of the bar smashing a mirror and some beer glasses. The bottle barely missed Patrick Carlisle who swiftly hit the deck to avoid the impact. Carlisle became furious and leapt in the direction of Jerry, grabbed him by the collar and gave him two super-fast slaps across the face.

After he received his scolding Jerry recovered immediately from his intoxication. Carlisle then went to the bar and grabbed a container filled with ice cold water. He went over to Jerry, who read what was happening and immediately ran for cover, but was not fast enough, he tumbled over some tables and fell flat on his back. When he opened his eyes he thought he was caught in a tsunami as the ice cold water made contact with his face. He made some gasping sounds as though oxygen was evading his nostrils, and then started to plea for mercy in a tone that made all the punters laugh. Jerry's pleading accent sounded like that of an aristocrat, and even Patrick Carlisle stole a secret smile, although he remained serious and committed to the task at hand. Carlisle went over to Jerry and pulled him from the ground, giving him two more slaps to make sure that he was awake and coherent, Carlisle then handed him his jacket, and told him that he was banned for life and ordered him to leave the pub. One-eyed Jerry reluctantly obeyed Carlisle's request, but not before spouting what sounded like a foreign language with some hints of bollocks..........bloody..........wanker. With that he exited the pub leaving behind a trail of destruction. Naturally he was back the following week.

⤬ 2 ⤬

PETER CARLISLE

Vic acquired *The Refuge by means* of a gambling debt owed to him by Peter Carlisle, the grandson of Patrick Carlisle. Vic was a very serious gambler who would stop at nothing to get what was owed to him. Peter Carlisle received a couple of broken bones before he gave in and surrendered the pub to Vic.

Peter Carlisle was a wannabe playboy who owned a lot of shares in the stock market. When he was living the aristocratic life, he used to date the fanciest girls in London. The girls would be drooling over him. He wore only designer suits and drove sports cars. He was like the real life James Bond if you like. He used to splurge on fancy dress parties where only the finest whisky and champagne was served.

Peter was a well-built bloke who had a narcissistic personality. He would spend hours at the gym trying to look his best for the ladies. Whatever he did was done solely to please the ladies. He saw himself as the most eligible bachelor in London Town. However, the good life was to be tarnished by the events of Black Monday when the stock market crashed.

The events of Black Monday, October 1987, caused a

dramatic fall in stock prices around the world and the United Kingdom was no exception. Peter lost everything; he had to sell his house and his fancy cars. His life turned into a total nightmare and he had to move into the flat above his grandfather's pub. He was so depressed that he wore the same suit for weeks. It was uncertain if he even showered. He was in total desperation and he had no choice but to do what he knew best, which was to use money to make money as a result of which he took up binge gambling. He won sometimes, but whenever he lost it meant that he would be in a great deal of trouble with the winner because he always tended to bite off more than he could chew.

Patrick Carlisle spotted the potential in Peter as a young lad. He knew that Peter had a good business head because he was always good at numbers and his memory was impeccable. From an early age he would stop by the pub after lessons to listen to the pub talk and to do chores for the punters. He used to save every penny of his money and spend it on merchandise to sell to the same punters who seemed to pay whatever price was quoted no matter how outlandish it was. Peter charged exorbitant prices for his wares. His clients never once complained, out of respect for Patrick Carlisle.

From an early age Peter knew that the only way he was going to live the life he desired was to get in on the stock market game. He would sit and wait for his uncle to finish the daily newspaper and then he would study the business and financial news. He would pay close attention to the events of the financial world and as such he learnt how to trade before setting foot on a trading platform. He saved enough money to pay for his training in commodities trading. He took up a position with a small trading firm and from there his eyes were set on the top layer of the cake.

Patrick Carlisle, now a very old man, admired the independent nature of his grandson. He knew that he could leave the pub in a safe pair of hands as Peter was demonstrating all the qualities that he saw in himself when he was at the same age and by that time he had gained his independence. He would work long hard hours at the docks with his eyes set on owning a trading post which he soon acquired.

While his grandfather was alive, Peter was a respectable young man. When his grandfather died Peter was very sad, but he knew that Patrick Carlisle lived a very long and eventful life. He showed his love for his grandson by leaving his beloved 'Refuge' in his care.

Peter had no idea how to run a pub. Even though he used to hang around daily, he never learnt the core of the business, and was unable to uphold the image his grandfather built over the decades. He operated the pub more like a casino, than a quiet and peaceful drinking establishment. He would run back door gambling games that had very high stakes. The minimum entry fee for entering those games was a thousand pounds, no exception and money up front. Peter was never good at gambling, even though he was a very smart bloke he couldn't outsmart the sharks who saw gambling as a source of income. The back room tables would normally attract gangsters and the worse type of maggots in London. Peter normally steered clear of the high stake games and only collected a fraction from each winning as a dividend for hosting the game.

When he lost all his money on the stock market he had no choice but to start taking part in the games, to keep up appearances. Within no time his savings started to depreciate and he took up binge drinking. He could no longer hide his desperation as he always seemed intoxicated and was slowly becoming incoherent. He was a pitiful sight.

The pub stock was depleted and the once beautiful 'Refuge' needed a refuge itself. The paint was stripping, the roof started to leak and the establishment became a spider's paradise. The only activity taking place at the pub was the illegal gambling. From the outside, the pub looked as though it had been closed down for years which made the location more attractive to the maggots and germs of East London.

Peter was warned never to gamble with 'Vic the Slick', as Victor Montgomery was referred to in the gambling world. Vic had him on his knees, within a few minutes of the poker game, but was satisfied with a few IOUs for the time being. Months passed and Peter could not come up with the twenty thousand pounds owed to Vic. Vic contacted his enforcer Randy as soon as he reached the conclusion that Peter couldn't pay.

Randy was a beast of a man. He had a very coarse voice that roared even when he was whispering. His teeth were like charcoal with not even a spot of white in sight. He had a laugh that was so annoying it made a hyena sound musical. He had muscles shaped like huge cannonballs. He had a gut that made a woman who was nine months pregnant look as if she was in the initial stages of her pregnancy. In contrast to Randy, Vic was a slender, medium built stick of a man. The scariest part of his appearance was his face. He looked like a mean lion that hadn't eaten any meat in months. His face was hard and bony and his smile was nowhere in sight.

The only protection Vic had was Randy and Francis, (his overweight pit-bull) who seemed to weigh more than Vic himself. The most dangerous thing about Vic was his conniving nature and his ability to plan and get away with heists.

It was a cold morning when Vic and Randy went to take Peter for a ride. Randy did not even knock on the door he kicked it right in. Peter was still in bed when he felt the mattress flying across the room like a magic carpet. He was made to sign over the pub, with a few loose bones for persuasion. The men left him still wrapped up in his blanket not knowing if he was dead or alive.

'If he does not die, it will take him years to recover from that thrashing,' muttered Randy.

'Either way, he no longer owns a pub,' said Vic in a bold tone. It was then and there that Vic became the proud owner of the now broken-down 'Refuge'.

✂ 3 ✂

VIC MONTGOMERY

Vic wasn't always a slimy bastard. He once had a normal family life with a wonderful wife, Angie and twin sons Adam and John. Angie was Scottish with long blonde hair; and eyes as blue as the ocean. Her smile could fill an entire room and her effervescence was supreme. She kept Vic focused and sane, but could not curb his binge drinking. Adam and John were exact replicas of their parents. Adam looked like his father with dark hair and brown eyes, but without the bony face. John had blonde hair and blue eyes just like his mother.

The twins were about eight years old on that tragic Christmas night when their car collided with a lorry. The family was returning from Christmas dinner where Vic had too much brandy to drink. Despite Angie's concern about his state of intoxication, Vic insisted that he could man the wheel. The scene of the accident was horrific. The two boys died on the spot, while Angie received massive injuries to her head and both legs broken. Vic did not even receive a scrape.

Angie lay in a vegetative state for about three months before she died. Vic stayed by her side throughout her hospitalization and after her death, tried committing suicide unsuccessfully on several occasions. Once he tried to hang himself, but the rope was not strong enough. Another time he tried to electrocute himself in the bath, but got cold feet at the last minute.

He was found guilty of manslaughter and served ten years in prison. The judge sentenced him to thirty years, but it was shortened due to a well-orchestrated plea of insanity. He spent five years in the Bedlam Mental Institution and was then released.

⤬ 4 ⤬

BEDLAM

In *Bedlam, Vic met a lot of loony's* who had done some ridiculous things in their lifetimes. He knew that he wasn't exactly crazy and had to remind himself constantly of this fact. Five years was a very long time to play the role of a crazy man. Instead of inventing an imaginary friend, Vic learnt the art of splitting himself like Jekyll and Hyde. He developed a virtual world in his mind where Jekyll was the good guy and Hyde was the antagonist. He often switched characters to ensure that he maintained a mental balance. He didn't want to get stuck with either of these characters because Vic was still very active in the virtual world. Vic played the role of the moderator so as to ensure that neither Jekyll nor Hyde went overboard and did something stupid that would cause him to be stuck at Bedlam for the next decade. When Vic was bored he would pit Jekyll and Hyde against each other just for entertainment, however, he would normally intervene when they were becoming too overwhelming. They would occasionally slip out in public and Vic couldn't have that because he didn't want to be labeled as having multiple personality disorder, which would mean that he, may never see the light of day again. A disorder of this nature would be seen as a risk to society because it is difficult to contain a person with this ailment.

Vic was a bloke who had foresight, so he could plot his moves far into the future. While at Bedlam, he designed a thirty-year plan that would ensure he ended up with enough money to secure a nice and comfortable future. Hyde was responsible for carrying out the sinister side of the plot and Jekyll was responsible for the strategic side of things while Vic himself was the voice of reason and logic. When Hyde's input was seen as too outlandish, Vic was responsible for erasing it from his thoughts and from his memory so as to ensure that it didn't pop up in the future. With these two virtual friends, Vic knew that if he kept it up one would dominate the other and he may have to choose which one to keep and which one to eradicate completely from his mind. Deep down he knew that Hyde would be ideal for the adventure that he would embark on when he got out. He also admitted to himself that his true personality was similar to that of Jekyll; therefore, Jekyll would no longer be needed. Vic promised himself that he would only bring out Hyde when it was completely necessary. Vic knew that he wasn't a very good fighter he couldn't even throw a decent punch. However, if he needed to do some proper work on somebody he would commission Hyde to deliver the payload.

Vic spent the remainder of his time at Bedlam learning how to control Hyde. At first it was a very difficult battle because Hyde was by nature stronger than Vic. With learning how to control Hyde, Vic grew stronger as a person. This was necessary because he couldn't allow a figment of his imagination to take him over completely. He learned how to switch Hyde on and off like a car engine. He could put him in overdrive if he wanted or cruise at a moderate speed. Vic also devised a way to get rid of Hyde when he no longer needed him. To do this, Vic knew that he would have to erase his own memory; even the memory of his loving family who were now floating in heaven would be lost forever. Vic wasn't all that bothered because he still knew his real self and he was confident that old Vic would come up with a proper plan to ensure that all wouldn't be lost.

⋊ 5 ⋉

PENTONVILLE

Vic spent his ten years prison sentence at Pentonville *Adult* Correctional Institution. During his stay at Pentonville, he met a lot of undesirables, who taught him how to be slimy. He learnt all the tricks of the trade. Vic was not a very brave man before he went to prison. He'd been beaten on several occasions before he met Randy. He was about to be hammered by the 350lb prison bully Big Mike when Randy, a man of similar build leapt in and took the knockout blow that was meant for Vic, literally saving his life. The blow barely moved Randy from where he was standing. Randy immediately answered Mike with an uppercut punch which connected to his throat. When Big Mike hit the pavement, it felt like a tremor measuring 4.1 on the Richter scale. Big Mike's larynx was almost smashed in. He tried to speak, but it seemed as if his voice box had been displaced and all he could do was hold his throat and moan in agony. The bully was defeated and all the prisoners in the yard cheered.

From that day until now, Vic knew he was safe with Randy by his side. Vic knew he had the perfect sidekick to help him execute his plans once they got out of prison. Vic's plan was to get involved in anything that would make him money. Since Angie died he decided to embark on a carefree existence with the sole aim being to make a ton of money, either by legal or illegal means. Vic didn't have the muscle, but he had the brain and patience to ensure that his plans followed through.

When Vic was being transferred from Pentonville to Bedlam, Big Mike made a vow and a promise that he would one day have his revenge. As he watched Vic getting away, he steamed. He appeared to have been transformed into the Incredible Hulk, and the only consolation would have been tearing the bars apart, grabbing Vic and strangling him.

⚔ 6 ⚔

THE COCK FIGHT

Vic had a lot of enemies, very dangerous blokes including loan sharks, pub landlords, gamblers and the Italians, the Mussolini brothers, who Vic owed twenty thousand pounds. The initial amount was ten thousand, but in the world of maggots the interest rate is calculated on an hourly basis, doubling it in no time. The Italians gave Vic a month to come up with the money or else.

Vic met the Mussolini brothers at a cockfight. The Italians were betting big on the most ferocious cock in town; called Little John. Little John was a very unpredictable bird, small but very dangerous. He had a fast and mean right foot and his spurs were razor sharp. Little John had over a hundred fights under his belt, no defeats and no draws. A real champion in his world Little John was. The Italians had over twenty thousand large on the table for Little John to win and they had the highest confidence in their bet for Little John was up against Lucky. Lucky was an average fighting cock that had won a number of fights, but he had no chance against Little John. The stakes were high and Lucky was the underdog and Vic loved it. Vic a master in deception knew exactly what to do to come out a winner. He decided he was going to rig the fight and was going to bet on the underdog and win.

Vic knew James Johnston commonly referred to as JJ the owner of Lucky. JJ was a drunk who could be convinced to do anything. He was an old man who had a limp similar to the Hunchback of Notre Dame. His limp was the result of a curved spine from years of bad posture. He had a beard and unexpectedly also an aristocratic accent. He always fancied himself to be a scientist and was always experimenting with all sorts of things and even claimed to have invented a time machine which took him to another era. What actually happened was that the machine fell over a precipice and the bottom was so dark he thought he was floating in the universe. For years he thought he had actually travelled to another era, until he admitted to himself that time travel only exists in the mind.

JJ started experimenting with fighting birds when he was running out of money. He realized that cockfights could make him a lot of quick cash. JJ figured out that he could enhance the deadliness of the cock's spurs to give it an advantage and started experimenting with poisonous chemicals which he would tip on the spurs in order to give the bird the extra edge it needed to dominate its opponents. JJ was not a greedy bloke, so he allowed his birds to be beaten on a few occasions. He didn't want to raise any suspicion especially, since the fights were always frequented by the maggots and germs of society. Vic went to JJ with the idea of rigging the fight. At first JJ was not willing to take any chances with this fight. He knew that the Italians and the Jamaicans had a lot of money on the table and that all the money would be on Little John to win. Everybody knew that Lucky would have to be extra lucky to beat Little John.

Eventually JJ agreed, so they had to figure out a way to

get the poison on the bird after all the checks were made. Vic knew that the spurs would be checked by the referees before the fight started and they decided that they were going to allow Lucky to be knocked around for a while before they applied the lethal poison to his spurs. No chances could be taken. The word was out that the Mussolini brothers had a load of money on the fight. Those guys could easily spot deception, and that's what had kept them alive all these years.

On the night of the fight JJ was very nervous because he knew that Lucky didn't stand a chance against Little John even with rigged spurs. Little John was built like an armored vehicle. Once he had been placed in the ring against three other birds and they gave him a proper thrashing. He almost lost all his feathers, but after the dust cleared he was the only bird standing. After that fight, Little John was treated like a king. He was on display like a trophy, and even wore a gold necklace with a huge pendant just like a superstar.

That night when Little John entered the venue, he was welcomed with screams and thundering applause. When Lucky entered the room, the air was filled with laughter and boos. The referee entered the ring as if he was a master of ceremony. He had on a high hat and a waist coat and looked like an undertaker ready to deliver the dead. He checked the two birds thoroughly for any foreign objects or substance. The birds were declared clean and the fight was ready to begin. The Italians were there and the Jamaicans were out in their numbers. Vic was studying the spectators with more interest in their facial expressions than in the fight itself. They seemed confident and their faces showed signs of expected victory and lined pockets.

Vic was wearing a disguise, for he knew that if he was spotted in the corner of the winning bird suspicion would be raised. This was because everybody knew about Vic and his sliminess; they knew that Vic never lost and he never played fair. If Vic is around foul play is not too far behind. His disguise was convincing as he was wearing a beard, a jacket and spectacles. He looked like Doctor Doolittle and his accent was similar to that of JJ's. He looked like a gentleman and his disguise was so good, not even JJ recognized him at first. He checked with JJ to ensure that he had the poison ready, as the plan was to apply the poisonous substance on Lucky's' spurs at the first opportune moment.

The fight got off to a nasty start and Little John was in his element as usual. He was giving it to Lucky left, right and center, and although Lucky managed to get in a couple of blows the acrobatic Little John was too quick; and the spurs barely got past his feathers. Lucky had taken a nasty blow to the head and was bleeding profusely. He seemed to be going down when JJ shouted for a time out. JJ took Lucky in his arms with tears falling down his cheeks. He knew that now was the time to apply the poison to his spurs, but first the bleeding needed some urgent attention. JJ reached for his whisky and gobbled down some before spitting the rest on the bird's face. The sensation of the whisky on the cuts on Luckys' face made him leap up as though he had just woken from a coma. The look in his eyes was ferocious, and even without the poison, JJ knew that Lucky was going to beat the shit out of Little John. When the fight resumed, Lucky was all over Little John. Lucky's first blow was aimed for the eyes and he got them both. Little John was now in total darkness and he was throwing potential blows in all directions, but Lucky was nowhere around. Lucky then went in with his left spur and it connected with Little John's throat. Little John fell flat on his back with his feet in the air, he was out cold and the fight came to an abrupt end.

Immediately after this happened Vic looked over at where the Italians were sitting. His eyes were in direct contact with those of Sergio Mussolini, but Vic wasn't sure if he recognized him or if he was saying goodbye to his share of the prize money. He just wasn't certain and he was not going to stick around to find out. Vic immediately went to collect his winnings and walked away with over thirty thousand pounds. Some of which belonged to the Italians and the Jamaicans.

Vic knew he was being followed that night, so he decided to spend the night at a bed and breakfast instead of taking the risk of going home to the pub. The next day he left through the back exit of the bed and breakfast and got rid of the disguise and decided to grab a cab just in case the car was being watched. The Italians and the Jamaicans already knew the description of the bloke that walked away with the top prize. They were looking for an old man with a beard and they had already paid JJ a visit, and he didn't have a clue what they were talking about thanks to the two bottles of whisky he drank celebrating Luckys' victory. The Italians insisted that there was some funny play and the Jamaicans agreed. Tony British, the leader of the Jamaicans decided to hold on to Lucky until he had some clear insight as to what the hell was going on. The Italians only needed a name, any name that would get them close enough to the bloke that took them for a ride. They decided that they were going to keep a close eye on JJ. They knew that JJ must have had some help to pull off something as big as rigging a fight with so much at stake. They watched JJ for weeks until one day they spotted Vic entering JJ's 'lab'. The Mussolini brothers immediately started to add up the situation and realized that Vic had something to do with the cockfight. From that moment Vic was placed on their books as a debtor.

The Mussolini brothers put the debt at ten thousand pounds, half of what they lost at the fights. The interest on this debt was to be calculated at an hourly rate. This means that ten thousand could easily be turned into fifteen thousand by the time they caught up with Vic.

⚯ 7 ⚯

THE MUSSOLINI BROTHERS

The Mussolini brothers came to London in the seventies after escaping the Sicilian mafia war, to find refuge. They were honest for a couple years before they decided to embark on a life of crime and mayhem. Silvio was the elder brother by two years. He had jet black hair that he always combed backwards. He had a long bony face and a very serious disposition. The younger was Sergio. He had a remarkable resemblance to his brother except he was a bit shorter. Sergio was the enforcer whereas Silvio acted as negotiator, or the voice of reason, if you like. They both liked to wear dark suits and silk shirts.

When they had first arrived they got some work on the docks. Life was very hard in those days. They had to work long hours in the blistering cold. They were practically doing slave labor. Their earnings were only enough to keep their bellies full and their bodies warm. The brothers lost their jobs along with hundreds of other workers due to the global economic meltdown of the 1970s when many docks and factories were forced to close. As a result of the latter, 1970s East London developed a landscape of dereliction and decay. The only jobs available were in the mines located miles away. The

Mussolini brothers worked the mines for a few months, after which they came to the conclusion that they weren't going to make it in life by doing this strenuous manual labor. They did some gambling, on the side, before they became loan sharks, eventually setting up a café as a front for their illegal activities. By the eighties, the Mussolini brothers had a hand in every underground activity in London. They had a stake in everything from high street stores to garbage disposal. They were organized, well established, and were well known by the Old Bills. Their business acumen which appeared honest overshadowed their underworld activities. In the eyes of everyone, they were honest hardworking business men.

The Mussolini brothers loved money, and would stop at nothing to get what was owed to them. They decided that they would pay Vic a little visit and make him an offer he couldn't refuse.

Vic was standing at the bar when the brothers entered the building, and he almost fainted when he saw them coming over to him. He knew instantly that something was wrong because they had never visited his establishment before. Instead of walking up to him, they changed direction, going over to the other side of the bar and ordered a couple shots of whisky. Looking over at Vic they acknowledged him with identical nods. Vic nodded back and asked if he could be of help to them. Silvio Mussolini looked over and said 'As a matter of fact you can. We are interested in investing some money in your establishment, and by the looks of things it obviously could use a face lift.'

Vic was enraged by this remark. He was now aware that the brothers knew about his involvement at the cockfight. That's the only reason they would pay him a visit like this. The scariest part of it was that the Mussolini brothers were winding him up. They were acting as if they had no knowledge of him rigging the cockfight.

He asked, 'Why do you blokes want to invest in a worthless place like this?'

Silvio's response was, 'We just want to go into the liquor business, and we feel your place has a lot of potential, although the appearance is rather neglected at present.'

'Get the hell out of my pub, you wankers!' shouted a now defensive Vic. Randy was at the other side of the bar and couldn't help but notice that Vic was crying out for help by the SOS expression on his face.

Randy immediately went over and roared, 'What the hell is going on here Vic?'

'Nothing Randy' stated Vic. 'Only these losers are trying to strong-arm me.'

'I suggest you guys go on your way....' Before Randy could finish his statement, he

was staring down the nostrils of a shotgun. Silvio now had a sly smirk on his face. The pub was clear with the first crank of the shotgun. Vic and Randy were left standing alone with the Mussolini brothers, and their big bad shiny friend.

'Are you ready to talk business?' asked Silvio.

'We are all ears,' answered Vic.

'You thought you were so slick that night at the cockfight in your little disguise,' stated Sergio. 'You stole some money from us and we want it back, Vic.'

'Although you thought you could get away with it, we are smarter than you,' stated Silvio. 'We found out that you were mates with JJ, and we knew he didn't have the balls to pull off something so daring. We lost twenty thousand pounds that night, but decided we only want back ten thousand; however, the interest on the ten thousand is another ten thousand. Therefore, you now owe us twenty thousand.'

'We are giving you a week from today to pay us the money. If your debt isn't cancelled by the end of the week we will burn this place down with you in it.' Sergio threatened.

The Mussolini brothers left immediately after without saying another word.

Vic turned to Randy and asked, 'Why didn't you do something? You bloody coward!'

'I may be big, but I am not made of steel,' answered Randy.

Vic said, 'We are in a very tough situation here.'

'I know,' replied Randy. 'However we have another, more urgent matter to take care of.'

'What are you talking about?' inquired Vic.

'Do you remember Big Mike?

'Yes, of course. What about him.'

'Well, I heard that he is coming to town to pay us a visit.

⋈ 8 ⋈

BIG MIKE

When *Big Mike's tenure at Pentonville* was up, he promised Randy that he would never forget him and Vic no matter how many years passed, he would always remember their names. This promise left a bad taste in Randy's mouth because he knew that Big Mike had some IRA affiliation and the entire population at Pentonville knew that Big Mike was a very dangerous bloke. He did not suppress the fact that he could do some really bad things.

Big Mike was born in London to an Irish mother and an English father. He lived in London until he was a teenager. His father died of throat cancer when he was fourteen years old; some people say that he binged on the 'deadly poison' which led to his death. If by chance you are wondering what the deadly poison is, it is the mixture of tobacco and hard liquor such as whisky, vodka and all the other spirits that have a high concentration of alcohol. It must also be said that the smog that hovered over London in those days was also a contributing factor.

After Big Mike's father passed away life began to prove too difficult for his mom to cope. Even though Mike was an only child his mother found it really hard to put bread on the table. It was rumored that she had engaged in prostitution in Soho. The kids in the neighborhood would tease and hound him on a daily basis. The bullying and the harassment led Mike to become a recluse and he started packing on the pounds which led to more bullying. The only solution Mike had to this problem was to retaliate and kick their asses. Eventually Mike became the aggressor at school and he was branded a bully. Mike's mother did not have any relatives in London and his father's family was nowhere to be found.

His mother decided that the only way to escape the suffering was to move back to Belfast where her parents and a number of siblings resided. At first, Mike didn't want to move to Ireland because he was now the king of his school and his neighborhood. He feared that if they moved he would be bullied all over again. His mother eventually convinced him to go to Belfast and so he did.

Upon arriving in Belfast, Mike found that he had many cousins with similar body statures to his own. The resemblance was uncanny, Mike had a huge tummy and so did his cousins. Mike felt that they had a lot in common and with that notion he started to relax. Mike's experience and his cousins' enthusiasm to learn about London, quickly gave him leverage to become the leader of the pack.

As they grew into adults their appearance transformed from fat to muscle, and they started to look like bouncers. They formed a successful criminal organization that consisted solely of family members, and they went by the name 'The Throat Smashers'. As the name suggests, they would go around smashing the throats of their rivals. Mike always wore a leader band around his hand that was adorned with spikes. Just the thought of getting smashed by Mike would at times have the rivals running.

The Throat Smashers operated a thriving extortion business in Belfast. It proved a success because the police had their attention elsewhere trying to take down the IRA. The Throat Smashers even had their own uniform so that their activities would seem legal. They were seen as a special police force for the area, which guaranteed the protection of all the shop owners within a twenty miles radius of their domain.

The other side of the twenty miles radius belonged to the most feared gang in Belfast 'The Headache Crew'. Their activities were also synonymous with their name. They gave the residents of Belfast one constant headache by wreaking havoc, and even the police feared them. A special task force was mobilized to take down 'The Headache Crew', but it proved difficult because they were very secretive, most of the members didn't even know each other. The gang spread like a plague throughout Belfast and they were right on the door steps of Big Mike's Gang. Big Mike was bothered by this because he knew that his Throat Smasher gang was outclassed and outnumbered. Once he tried to merge the two factions but it proved futile because they couldn't come up with the best solution on how to share power.

The leader of 'The Headache Crew' was called 'Ground God', who felt he was invincible. He would park his car anywhere without fear of theft, and never paid for anything; as he had the 'Keys to the City'. Ground God was the supreme leader, the governor, the judge and the executioner of Belfast. He kept a low profile and many people didn't even know his face, but his moniker alone evoked fear in their hearts.

Big Mike knew that it was only a matter of time before Ground God and his crew launched an assault on his twenty miles radius. The Throat Smashers decided that they had to pre-empt The Headache Crew by launching the first attack. Understandably, he was nervous about the inevitable attack. On one occasion he accidentally shot his cousin Big Jim in the leg because he thought someone else was sneaking up on him. Luckily it was just a flesh wound and Jim survived. After this incident Big Mike decided that it was time for action and told his soldiers to prepare for war. He remembered the old western movies with the Indians; and what the cowboys did to stop an Indian uprising was to take out the Chief. Big Mike then reached the conclusion that only one shot needed to be fired and he would have to be the bloke to make the delivery. He figured that if he took out 'Ground God', 'The Headache Crew' would be destroyed.

At Big Mike's behest a meeting was arranged with 'Ground God'. He made 'Ground God' believe that the meeting was to merge the two gangs, and assured 'Ground God' leadership. This meeting was to take place at an abandoned warehouse by the Belfast harbor. Big Mike sent a small contingency of soldiers two days in advance to scout out and secure the meeting place. He knew that he could not take any chances with the serpent 'Ground God'. Mike knew all too well that 'Ground God' would undoubtedly have something up his sleeve, and the meeting would no doubt turn out to be a bloody massacre.

The encounter was to take place under the cloak of darkness, just in case the authorities caught wind of it. Big Mike was already at the docks when Ground God's motorcade rolled in. His jaguar was in the middle protected by two jeeps on either side. He was treated like a king and his men were almost fighting to open the door, when he took out his cigar the darkness was illuminated by lighters, all vying to be the first to light the Cuban.

The two men embraced each other to show their respect, and to paint a picture that they were reasonable men who were able to sit down and have a civilized discussion about who should take the lead. The embrace however, was very brief, and as soon as the men parted their faces became grim as the rivalry had only been put aside for a moment. The discussion was mainly about territory and the free access to each other's domain if there was to be any sort of power sharing. 'Ground God' was not pleased with the sharing of the territory clause because he controlled almost the entire city except Mike's twenty miles domain.

'I can smash you right here, right now, where you stand Mike!' said Ground God with a flushed face.

'I just want to see you try,' replied Mike with flaming eyes.

'I can put you to the ground right now and your men won't be able to do anything about it!' Ground God shouted.

Mike now had a sinister look on his face. Ground God immediately started to look around. 'Look harder, you are surrounded by my men and you are at my mercy. I have you all pinned down, so don't make any funny moves.' Ground God now started to show signs of fear. Big Mike knew that he could not let Ground God see another day; he had to put him down right then and there. Without any warning a double barrel shotgun previously concealed under his trench coat surfaced.

When Ground God saw the nozzle of the gun his jaw dropped like that of a cartoon character, he could not believe he had been outsmarted by Big Mike! As soon as Mike cocked his weapon you could hear the chorus of other shotguns following suit in the quiet night. Ground God and his men were surrounded, so he fell to his knees and started to beg for mercy, but Mike knew that if he let him go he would come after him with all his strength. Big Mike closed his eyes and squeezed the trigger. Ground

God's body was blown to pieces and in all directions where he had been kneeling. After he had been blown away you could hear the singing of the other shotguns, and the tune was death.

After the massacre Big Mike knew that he had to skip town, so he left for London the same night with no intention of looking back. He arrived in London with a substantial amount of money, but in no time it had been depleted, trying to buy himself a name in the ever competitive London town. Before his money was almost finished, he mustered a small crew mainly consisting of wannabe criminals and petty thieves. They were so desperate that they tried to rob a church, and when the vicar intervened, Big Mike beat him unconscious. The vicar subsequently developed permanent amnesia, and could no longer serve his parish having to now be cared for constantly. When the Old Bill caught up with Mike he was trying to steal a car. The cops investigated then found out that he was behind several robberies including the assault on the vicar. Mike was sentenced to fifteen years at Pentonville and that's where he met Vic Montgomery and Randy.

⊰ 9 ⊱

THE PAYBACK

Big Mike is now free and the promise he made to Vic and Randy still stood. Of his cousins that were still alive he summoned the four most loyal ones, to come immediately to London, to help him sort out some 'unfinished business'. He told them that they should bring all the tools they could round up, because it would be a potential replay of what happened at the docks with Ground God and his crew. Nothing more needed to be said. The cousins knew that they were going to London to do a job and they frankly didn't care about whom and why, they were only concerned about where and when.

Big Mike started to put his plan in action, watching Vic closely and studying his movements. He knew exactly what he did on a daily basis, and he could not wait to get his revenge. It was all he could do to patiently wait for the opportune moment to strike. He didn't want to get jumpy and things went badly. He wanted the job to be as professional as possible, without a trace. He definitely didn't want to go back to prison, so it had to be clean and precise.

Big Mike decided that he was going to get Vic, even if he had to burn down the pub with him inside it. He figured that Randy was a soft target, so the job on him did not require an intricate plan, but Vic would be a bit trickier. Big Mike knew that Vic was as crafty as they come, and he was always aware of his surroundings. He would be sure to notice anything odd or out of place.

Big Mike's bloodthirsty cousins arrived the following day, eager and ready to assist their cousin Mike. They still had a lot of respect for him for he was a legend in Belfast. The events at the docks had become folklore. Some of the more gory details were of course omitted from the story. They wanted to portray Mike in a good light as a liberator. After all, he got rid of Belfast's biggest 'headache'.

The four cousins told Big Mike that they still had a lot of influence in Belfast and it was safe for him to return any time he wanted. Every night, while in prison Big Mike dreamed of going back to Belfast. Surrounded by so much concrete, he longed to see the green of Ireland. He decided that he would return permanently after they terminated Vic and Randy.

Mike was holed up in a small budget hotel just outside London. He kept a low profile and the only time he left the room was when he went to stake out Vic and to grab a bite to eat. He made all his purchases with cash so as not to leave a trail. He gave the front desk clerk a false name, and his back was always turned to the security cameras. He did not want to be seen anywhere around town because he would be the first suspect in the case. It was common knowledge within law enforcement that the great prison bully was brought down to ground zero by Vic and Randy. Big Mike's plan was to get Vic and Randy then skip town immediately. He was going to be like the biblical Lot never looking back at the destruction behind him.

Vic started to watch his back after Randy told him that Big Mike had been released from Pentonville. Vic never forgot a promise and the one that Big Mike had made tormented him. It made him paranoid and untrusting. He kept Francis close to him when Randy was around and even closer when he was not around. Vic knew when Mike's cousins arrived and immediately started to devise a plan to strike first. He knew that Big Mike would not act alone, and from the moment he saw the reinforcements he knew that Mike meant business and was now in a position to make his move.

Vic shared his plans with Randy, who agreed that an immediate strike was a wise move. Mike would be caught off guard as he was unaware that Vic knew that he had been trailing him. The men agreed that they would need two more men to get the job done. There was no doubt that Big Mike and his associates had access to some heavy machinery. Randy had two mates, Fred and Harry who would be more than willing to partake in the 'festivities' if they were being paid the right amount of money. Randy immediately made contact and they both agreed to assist but only if Vic treated them with more respect and included them in other jobs. Vic agreed to give them more work and the men were satisfied with that.

Vic did not trust Randy's mates. They seemed dodgy and for a bloke like Vic to say that, dodgy must have been printed all over them. He decided that it would be best if Fred and Harry only knew the minor details of this plan and all others.

Vic and Randy devised a method how to get Big Mike before he got them. Fred and Harry would be there for additional firepower and also to act as bait. Vic was never an instigator, he preferred to be a mediator and he wasn't the type of guy to enter a building, a car, a room or anywhere first. He liked to enter when he knew the area was safe and then would do all the talking. However, there was not going to be a conversation with Big Mike. It was going to be an orchestra playing bullets, the finale being death.

The plan was made and the times confirmed. The band of men entered the hotel lobby with a collected composure, but inside eager to play their tune. The atmosphere was calm so they would play silently and professionally for one night only, then they would disappear into oblivion. Randy kicked the door in; the men entered and found a silent adversary.

✕ **10** ✕

THE OLD BILL

Detective *Elizabeth Somerset and* Detective Alex Dawson were the first to arrive on the scene. They knocked on the door only to be greeted by silence. They were still not sure who had made the call. DCI Dawson called out, 'This is the police, open the door!' Again the response was silence. They realized that it was too quiet, and Dawson decided to kick the door in, again announcing their presence, but the silence seemed even more eerie.

The detectives emerged from the foyer to find two men sitting before the television facing a blank blue screen. The men appeared to be fast asleep. Indeed they were... they were in a permanent slumber. Their heads were tilted backwards almost hanging over the back of the chair. They appeared not to have known what hit them and must have been caught off guard. Upon closer inspection, the detectives picked up the scent of chloroform. They surmised that the men must have been asleep when their attackers entered the room.

'They were rendered unconscious and then strangled.' said Dawson. 'It is quite obvious as they both have identical marks around their necks, suggesting that a wire had been used.' He looked at his partner and continued, 'The suspects obviously had been very silent because the other residents in the building seemed unaware of the mayhem that had gone down.'

The anonymous call was still bothering Dawson because the witness had called his private number. Someone obviously wanted him on the case. He went on to figure that it must have been one of the perpetrators who made the call, and decided that he would run a trace when he returned to the station. The method of execution made Dawson conclude that the hit men must have been professionals.

DCI Somerset saw what appeared to be a trail of blood at the entrance to the small kitchen. She went over and discovered a body lying face down in a pool of blood. It was obvious that he had been hit from behind. She figured that the man must have heard something, reached the kitchen door leading to the living room, saw what was happening, turned to run away and was hit in the back with a sawn-off shotgun. This was evident from the large hole in his back. The force of the impact sent the victim flying and his blood splattered everywhere.

The body count was at three, when DCI Somerset heard Dawson calling out from the bedroom. The detective entered the room to discover a king sized bed with what appeared to be crimson sheets. Upon closer inspection she realized that, it was a blood soaked blanket. A fourth man had been obliterated in his sleep. The expression on his face suggested that he had been having a pleasant dream.

The detectives moved carefully so as to ensure that they did not contaminate the scene. Dawson was now on his phone making a call to the station. He explained what he was seeing and shortly after you could hear sirens coming in their direction. He had to end the call abruptly, as he instinctively responded to screams coming from the direction of the foyer. He found DCI Somerset with her hands over her mouth trying to stop herself from vomiting. It was a fifth victim. A man, very large in stature was, sitting on the toilet still in the position of making a deposit. It was a very disgusting scene, even Dawson quivered.

The detectives immediately vacated the crime scene when the forensics team arrived. They were eager to get started on the case. The macabre nature of the killings left a bad taste in DCI Somerset's mouth. It was the worst experience in her recollection, and made her more aware of the darker side of life.

⌖ 11 ⌖

DETECTIVE ELIZABETH SOMERSET

Elizabeth Somerset joined the force at an early age. It still baffles people why such a beautiful, polished woman would want to be on the beat. The reality was that Elizabeth was as fierce as a tiger; and even though she was a deadly woman, she had a humanitarian side. She had to do something to uphold the values of society and the only thing she knew was to be tough both physically and emotionally. She had two brothers that took a liking to boxing at an early age and they helped to toughen her up. Elizabeth's father was a sailor and her mother was a school teacher from the Caribbean. She spent some time there but moved to England when she was a teenager. She did not fit in at first, but she eventually successfully positioned herself in the new land and she became strong and focused. She studied criminal psychology at university and was poised for success. She knew exactly what she wanted and she knew exactly how to get it. She moved up the ranks quickly and she was a brilliant burst of potential on all fronts.

Elizabeth was determined to catch the killers, being a woman of conviction and as stubborn as hell, she would hunt them down like animals. She got started right away and although she loved putting puzzles together this case was more challenging than usual and it became an obsession. She was determined to crack the case and it would be the biggest challenge of her law enforcement career. She had never seen so many victims in one crime scene and the thought of the big bloke on the toilet seat still made her feel sick in the stomach.

The victims seemed to have been hardened criminals who had obviously served time behind bars. She decided to run checks, and found an extensive background of criminal history. The information found on the men could be used as an encyclopedia on criminality and barbarism. She narrowed the men down to London and discovered that Big Mike had spent time at Pentonville. She felt a thrill knowing she was now on the right track. The danger, the darkness, the restriction of prison and of prisoners appealed to her. So deciding to pay the Guv at Pentonville a visit, she made the call and set up the appointment.

She arrived at the prison early the next day and was escorted in by a guard who was obviously drooling. She made it a point of duty to be extra sensual on the day and she wore a short skirt with no stockings, so that her legs would be bare and this would help the men with their imagination. She would enjoy teasing the hungry bulls in their pens and she purposely moved in a sensual fashion. She relished the sounds of the men howling and hissing, and she inwardly smiled as they salivated. She was on a catwalk advertising her wares and her movements were purposeful and sexually appealing. She regained her professionalism as she entered the Guv's office.

'Tell me all that you know about Big Mike,' she ordered instantly. She had not realized that the Guv was an equally beautiful woman, with a pair of legs as alluring as hers.

'Beg your pardon,' the Guv replied. 'Who do you think you are speaking to young lady?'

Elizabeth finally had met her match. The two women stared at each other for what seemed like an eternity. They both had the same appeal; they both recognized something in each other. They were both strong willed, stubborn, and domineering.

The Guv pursed her lips and smiled and she said, 'Have a seat Detective, what can I do for you today?'

'I am investigating a mass murder and the scent has led me here.'

'Oh, how fascinating,' said the Guv dryly.

'I would like some information about one of your previous residents, Big Mike, who served time here and was recently released.'

Elizabeth had now grasped the Guv's interest and she sat up straighter in her chair concentrating intensely.

She said, 'he stayed here before my time, but I have heard the stories, very interesting ones, as a matter of fact, they are now legends around here.'

'I want all the records you have on him, his pals, everything,' said Elizabeth in a confident tone.

'Well,' replied the Guv looking at her nails. 'The archives are all yours, have fun.'

Switching mood almost instantly, she added. 'Now get the hell out of my office, young lady! You need a lot more years under your belt before you could even start to think of ordering me around.' Scolding Elizabeth in a voice fragmented with laughter.

Getting up to leave Elizabeth asked in a more submissive tone, 'Where are the archives?'

'Down the hall to your left,' responded the Guv in an even softer tone. 'Tell Jim I sent you.'

The ladies gave each other a knowing smile and parted company.

The archive room was a cold and uncomfortable place. It was littered with cabinets stacked with files on villains and seemed to have been there since criminality began. Big Mike's files were found among the elites, the legends, the 'Old Boys'.

Big Mike's story intrigued Elizabeth. His files gave account of many altercations with a Vic Montgomery. For some reason the name rang an alarm bell in her head and sent shivers down her spine. She immediately shifted her attention to Vic and went in search of his file. Her eyes lit up when she found it. His story captivated her, and she had to know more about him. He did not seem to belong in this prison as he was not the hard and dangerous type. 'What was he doing here?' she asked herself. She grabbed the file and immediately exited the building; she knew she need not search any further for she felt that she had found 'the one'. She was a bit confused because there was no way of knowing if Vic was connected to the murders, but she was led to believe he did based on what she read about his history with Mike.

That night she made herself comfortable, and crawled under her sheets and read. She was touched by the tragedy of Angie and the boys. Her heart bled for him, but she knew that an event like this could make a man lose his soul searching for peace and comfort.

That thought of Vic Montgomery stayed in her mind. The next day she woke up extremely early, with butterflies in her stomach. She took up his file and stared at his picture and the initial alarm bells fell into place. She felt as if she knew Vic and then she remembered the compromised position she was in.

He had entered her life and she had not realized when she became trapped. His legacy, power and wealth restrained her. She recalled him speaking about a Victor and his desires to see him obliterated. The game was more dangerous than ever and she knew there were no fair play, no referee and no time outs. Big Mike now looked like his work and she felt like a pawn or bait. The trophy had been Vic Montgomery all along.

She decided to think deeply and came to a decision. She would arrest Vic for the murders and confess to her superiors. They would then free her from her bondage. She could trust no one, especially in the force, for he had far reaching tentacles. The best card for her to play was to proceed as normal, stay close to him, very close.

⊰ 12 ⊱

THE ABDUCTION OF FRANCIS

As *Vic approached the door* of his flat, still confused about what happened to Mike and his cousins, he was greeted with an unaccustomed silence. At first he couldn't place what was wrong but then realized he did not hear the familiar panting of Francis trying to breathe, through the layers of fat that covered his lungs. He called out his best friend's name, but all that ensued was that unwelcome silence. He ran to the bedroom but the dog was not there. He checked the bathroom, but still no Francis. He tried to suppress his fears but they threatened to overwhelm him. His eyes filled with tears, and he thought, 'what if?' Looking around some more, he checked the kitchen and discovered a package lying on the table. He opened it and took out an envelope. He quickly ripped it open eager to read the letter.

> *Dear Vic,*
>
> *We just wanted to make sure you understood the gravity of the situation. You owe us twenty thousand pounds, payable within forty eight hours. We sent you an extra ear to make sure you heard clearly what we said a few weeks ago when we came to visit. Looks familiar?*

Yours Truly,

Your friends from the cockfight

Before Vic could read another word, he dropped the letter and reached for the package. He put his left hand in and pulled out a right ear; a familiar ear, it belonged to Francis.

That night Vic wept for the first time since his life had been torn apart by the accident. Loneliness engulfed him and he felt weak and insecure. Francis was his best mate and his support when he was released from Bedlam. The dog helped him to get his marbles rolling in the right direction. He helped him to regain his emotions.

Revenge was on his mind and the scent of blood was still permeating through his nostrils. The image of Big Mike sitting on the toilet seat with a hole in his face came like flashes of lightning and his eyes burnt with fury. *'Should I hit them now or wait until I have formulated a plan?'* he thought. Rage said now, Reason said wait, and he listened to Reason. *'Could Francis be alive?'* He knew that the Mussolini brothers were two serious blokes and that he would now most certainly have to pay up if he wanted to see Francis alive again. There was no way he could raise the twenty thousand pounds in forty eight hours unless he robbed a bank and he was not foolish enough to do that. He could not put together that amount of money in the specified timeframe and the gambling tables were not turning over enough money. The players did not have much money to bet and most of the games were played for amusement purposes. One thing, for sure though, the players spent heavily on liquor. They left the pub every night with empty pockets and intoxicated minds. But even then he did not have enough liquor in stock to keep his patrons well watered.

Vic focused his thoughts and in came Hyde. He now had a plan and he could see the end before he had worked out the beginning. He reached the conclusion that the only way he could pay off the Mussolini brothers in time to save Francis was to bootleg whisky and use it to buy him some time while he flogged it. He was going to organize a heist, a 'Great whisky Heist,' the largest since the American Prohibition.

He knew he had to find the buyers before he sourced the product to ensure a quick sale. He had a hold on all the Off Licenses' in the area. They could not refuse his sale or else Randy would do a number on their place of business. The Off Licenses' however, could not take too much even if they were threatened with a gun. They did not have the space and their usual suppliers would become suspicious and Her Majesty's Revenues and Customs were always turning up unannounced to check that the duty has been paid on their liquor and cigarettes.

Vic knew he had to find some big buyers. He had to go wholesale and he knew exactly where to find those customers. He decided that he would also go down to the docks and talk to some exporters, who would be more than willing to relieve him of the merchandise for the right price.

✂ **13** ✂

WHEN VIC MET ELIZABETH

A *knock on the door interrupted* his thoughts. Cautiously *he* reached for his 9mm automatic. He peeped through the keyhole and saw two stunning legs standing on his steps and he quickly opened the door to have a look at the owner of the refined legs. He looked her over closely from the ground up. He looked deeply in her beautiful brown eyes and she stared back. His eyes caught her full lips still moist from the lip gloss that she had obviously just applied. She licked them gently and he immediately became hard. She noticed the bulge in his trousers and she smiled.

'Who are you?' asked Vic.

'I am DCI Somerset,' responded Elizabeth. 'I am investigating the murder of some people you might have known.'

'Did you come alone?' asked Vic in a sensual tone looking behind her.

'Yes, I did,' she replied.

'Is this a social call?' he smiled and asked.

'Why would it be a social call sir?' she asked.

'I would like it to be,' replied Vic.

'Well; it is certainly not a social call. I am on police

business,' responded Elizabeth. 'Are you going to let me in?'

'Excuse my manners. Come on in,' said Vic.

She entered the room and looked around the pub.

'Can I get you something to drink?' Vic asked coolly.

She replied, 'As I said before, this is not a social call.'

'Oh! Pardon my good hospitality. Offering to quench a fellow human being's thirst is certainly not a social call in my book,' said Vic.

Elizabeth ignored him and said, 'Five men were murdered recently in what looked like an act of revenge, a bit too messy, but the job was done.'

Vic was silent and he thought he better keep it that way.

She continued, 'It didn't take us long to connect you with the victims.'

'Who are the victims?' Vic asked with an innocent expression.

With a surprised look DCI Somerset said, 'you know Big Mike, you both received
your university education at the same institution. You dethroned him, making him the laughing stock of the general student population.'

Vic liked the way she used the phrase 'university education' for the word prison. He was in love, it was an instant attraction. He was mesmerized by her beauty and sternness. She was domineering and he liked that. She had an air of confidence that made her standout in any crowd. He knew that she was talking but he could not hear a word of what she was saying, because he was staring at her breasts.

'Snap out of it!' shouted Elizabeth, 'You are drooling like a baby. You men are so shallow and immature. You are all the same. If you had anything to do with these murders, I will prove it and bring you to justice.'

Vic enjoyed the way she walked away, he anticipated every step, and his extremity was once again aroused.

'Wait!' shouted Vic, finally breaking his silence. 'Sorry for seeming a bit dazed, someone nicked my dog and I am in mourning. Come back, let's talk.' His tone was smooth and calm and intended to evoke sympathy.

Elizabeth turned around and said, 'Are you going to confess? You may need to get in touch with your lawyer before you do.'

Vic kept wondering what else she knew. '*Has she been watching him? Maybe she had the entire Scotland Yard waiting outside.*' He stalled her, hoping to find out how much she knew about him. He knew his record was public, so there were no secrets about his character or his past, but did she know about his future?

He could not stop himself from staring. She had pouty lips that said, 'come on kiss me.' He went in for the kiss and she did not reject it, but he soon realized that she was not in his arms. He had been fantasizing and he stopped himself from violating her in reality. He knew that with such beauty and a gun, the consequences could be dire.

'Would you like a cuppa?' Vic offered.

'No thank you Victor, this is not a tea party,' she answered sternly.

'*No one has ever called me Victor, since Angie died,*' thought Vic. He started to become paranoid, but he decided to play it cool. He said, 'I have never seen you before; surely I could not have missed such beauty.'

'Oh, but I have seen you,' laughed Elizabeth. 'I have seen your record Victor and you have been a very naughty boy. The moment I saw your picture on your prison file I knew you looked familiar. I saw you at the cockfight where Little John lost both his eyes. Yes, I was there, that's where I go to observe the activities of the criminals in East London. I didn't remember at first, because you were in disguise, but you stood out. I must say I sort of admire you.'

Vic's heart skipped a beat when he heard her last words and he knew he must have her that night. He took a moment before he spoke again and another thought rushed in. *'Maybe this was indeed a social call, and she wanted to get herself some of this bad boy.'* His throat contracted with lust and he could not speak.

'It must be love at first sight,' the words finally escaped from his mouth.

'Who said anything about love?' Elizabeth asked. 'I just want to shag you and then arrest you.'

Vic was mesmerized by her boldness and began to salivate. His lips attacked hers with the fury and rage of a river smashing against its banks and this time it was real. She did not hesitate, her lip gloss was beginning to wear off and her lips needed to be moisturized. The pair could not hold back their emotions. Vic was seeing her for the first time, but she knew everything she needed to know about him. She was fulfilling a torturous desire for she knew that what she was doing went against everything that she believed in. That night she gave herself to him without hesitation and he ravaged her like a starving man.

The next day, Vic woke up with a pair of handcuffs around his wrists. He thought he was still having fun and this was a continuation of the party. Then the memory of her words came back to him, *'I just want to shag you then arrest you.'*

'She is really going to nick me.' he said to himself. He broke off the bed post that restrained him and hopped out of bed and surveyed his flat. She was gone, but he could still smell her essence. 'What does this mean?' he asked himself. He un-cuffed himself with the speed of an escape artist, grabbed his pants and ran from the flat. He jumped in his car and headed straight to Sam 'The Gun' McDougal's place.

⋈ **14** ⋈

SAM 'THE GUN' MCDOUGAL

Sam *'The Gun' McDougal, despite* his now worn-out appearance was actually an ex-SAS and master marksman. He was reared in the art of killing and was trained as a sniper. He could shoot the button from a jacket without damaging the jacket itself. He had been dishonorably discharged from the military after his drinking gradually changed from casual, to habitual and then binging. He no longer had a steady hand, which was the main criterion for being a sniper. Over the years, since his discharge, he had gone through a lot of misery and pain and as a result he had become an angry man. He was now very old and weathered. One of his abilities that had not faltered was his ability to run a business. He operated a successful garage that maintained and repaired mostly high end vehicles. A geezer had to be tough to stay in a business like that. The heavies around town including Vic would use the local garages to disguise stolen cars and Lorries. They would modify the cars and then use them to hide and haul stolen contraband.

The Old Bill caught wind of the operations and many garages were shut down. McDougal was completely overlooked because of his military past and high profile clients. However, this didn't stop the heavies from trying to muscle their way into his operation. At one point he had to barricade himself in, as some blokes tried to steal a couple of Jags from the premises. They were not aware that McDougal was sitting on an arsenal and he welcomed the opportunity to grease the machines.

The shootout lasted for what seemed like an eternity until the wee hours of the morning. They were all using silencers so the neighbors had no idea what was taking place, only a few meters down the road. McDougal was the only man standing after the smoke cleared. Mr. McDougal and his pistols did a fine job on the thieves and from that night no one dared disrespect Sam 'The Gun' McDougal. They knew that this guy was dangerous and even more so under the influence of whisky.

Everyone knew that McDougal killed the robbers, but it was played off as a gang against gang shootout that happened to take place on his premises. All the guns used in the shooting were melted down and thrown in the scrapheap. No evidence tied him to the crime and besides, he was drunk as hell. When the coppers arrived, they assumed that no way McDougal alone could have annihilated all the blokes lying outside in their own blood.

He was hungry, business was not doing well and he needed a break. He was as clean as a whistle, but now he was desperate. He was a very savvy businessman, but he could not keep the garage going through the rough times. He was now faced with stiff competition from the newer and more modern garages. Most high end vehicle manufacturers were now putting up their own garages to service their brand of vehicles and they were offering large discounts to their clients. People could now get vehicles on hire purchase where they would only have to pay in installments and the after sale service included maintenance and repairs.

Now losing valuable business, he had to diversify his operation, so he invested in a fleet of Lorries which he rented out to people moving house. He would many times even do some removal himself. He was now known as the 'nice van guy'. He also had a couple of larger lorries which he contracted out to do intercontinental haulage. Business for him was steady. The money was still coming in, but he had introduced austerity measures on many things but not including his beloved whisky, he would rather stop eating than stop drinking. Even though business was moderate, he still saw the intake as mediocre and he missed the touch and feel of the Mercs and Jags.

McDougal was one of Vic's most loyal customers and he also considered him a friend. He was at the pub every night. As a matter of fact he spent most of his nights there, literally. He was always too drunk to get home and besides, he was always the last patron left. He was also quite friendly with Francis who sometimes offered his services as a guard dog to McDougal's garage when Vic was out of town.

Francis may have been an obese animal; however, his bark could scare the hell out of anyone. McDougal realized this and kept him indoors. Francis would sound the alarm when he heard strange noises but all he could do was bark for he had no speed. If the robbers around town knew this, they would tear the place down every night. Even though the dog was not there all the time, McDougal devised a way to still keep the 'Francis Effect' going. He recorded Francis' most ferocious bark and the strange noises he made and played it over the speaker system he had installed. The sounds were so ferocious one could envision the dog's rage with saliva dripping from his mouth. It was McDougal's red alert system, and it proved very effective.

He was extremely angry when Vic told him what had happened to Francis, for he loved the animal dearly. Vic saw fire in his eyes and he knew that McDougal would do anything to avenge his beloved Francis. Vic told McDougal that the Mussolini brothers were behind the abduction and it made him very angry. He did not care too much for Italians for they had joined forces with the Germans in World War Two. He saw this as an opportunity where Vic was giving him his heart's desire on a silver platter. He was out for blood and the Italians would provide it. After the war he had volunteered to hunt down the Germans who found refuge in friendly countries. He hunted them from Asia to South America. He received many honors and medals for his service to the crown. However, they all meant nothing after the memories of the war became overwhelming and he started drinking. He was stripped of all his medals and he was isolated.

⋈ **PART II** ⋈

THE GREAT WHISKY HEIST

⪥ 15 ⪥

THE JOURNEY TO SCOTLAND

Vic shared his plans with Mcdougal, carefully emphasizing the points that would most certainly get his attention. Vic made it clear to McDougal that he was doing it for Francis. The Mussolini brothers held him hostage and the heist was the only way he could get him back. With the thought of Francis hurt, McDougal immediately agreed to provide the transportation and hardware for the heist. All he was concerned about was getting back at the Mussolini brothers by any means necessary, even if he had to drive hundreds of miles to Scotland and back. He just wanted to get close to them and that would only be possible when the exchange was made, the liquor for the dog. He promised Vic that he would personally handle the matter and he would get to it right away.

Vic was happy that McDougal had been receptive to his plans, as he knew that somewhere beyond his current state of fury and intoxication he was still savvy and could not be misled. The lorries would be clean and Vic was relieved by the fact that he would not have to resort to stealing. Vic did not know that McDougal intended to make the journey to Scotland as well. McDougal went into a long and rather boring reminiscence of the old days and how long he had waited to kiss the shores and mountains of Scotland. He was now keen on making the journey not for the heist that would guarantee the release of his beloved Francis, but for the memories. Vic could not bear the nostalgia any longer and he had to give in to McDougal just to avoid the long trip down memory lane.

Once McDougal got the green light, he immediately went into military mode on Vic. 'Logistics...check, food supply...check, survival kit...check, hardware...check.'

Vic now had a curious look on his face. He then barked the question at McDougal, 'Hardware?'

'Yes, you can't trust those bloody Scots. I should know I am one of them. Besides who knows Vic, you may just run into some of your old pals who I am sure would be very happy to see you. After what happened with Angie and the boys, I am sure you don't have many friends up there and I can assure you I don't have many friends there either. Furthermore, if, and when, trouble comes knocking, you must be ready and able to deal with it, using the right tools,' answered McDougal aiming the old rifle around the room.

Vic now felt pushed into a corner. McDougal's reasoning hit a note especially with the mention of Angie and the boys. It sent a wave of memories rushing into his mind, which consisted of guilt and emptiness. 'Ok, but travel light I don't want to get done for possession plus armed robbery. This is meant to be a clean job, just in and out like a ghost,' Vic scolded McDougal.

'Ok Vic, I hear you,' responded McDougal in a sarcastic sounding submissive tone.

'So what's the next move?' he enquired.

Vic made a call summoning Randy to McDougal's place, and he instructed him to bring along his two stragglers, Harry and Fred. He never trusted those two blokes, but he trusted Randy. He relied on Randy's judgment and his huge right hand. Randy must have seen something of value in them; otherwise he wouldn't have kept them around for so long. They must have been two of the most cunning and thieving bastards in the East End. They could steal the hands off Big Ben and still make it tick. Vic was a bit reserved in bringing them in on the action, but he desperately needed manpower and drivers. The journey to Scotland had to be worthwhile, the shipment would have to be huge, and the plan was to wipe out at least three distilleries and it would not be an easy task. The danger involved had to be noted, for the brewers in Scotland were always on the lookout for whisky thieves. They had dogs and lots of heavy metal.

Randy turned up within thirty minutes of his summons, with his two stragglers, straggling behind as usual. Vic gave a brief synopsis of the plan and the men got the transportation ready.

As they were about to mount up Tony British arrived at the garage looking for McDougal. He had a problem with the chassis on his car and he ordered McDougal to look at it. He spotted Vic and a serious look took over his face. He said, 'What are you doing here Vic?'

'Minding my own bloody business and you should too,' replied Vic sternly.

Tony British ignored him and turned his attention to the other men and the lorries with their engines running. He said, 'I see you are going on a little road trip. I can't keep my eyes off you one minute. I am going to kill that bastard who was supposed to be watching you.'

Vic thought for a moment and realized that he could use an extra pair of hands and besides Tony British was not as dangerous as he seemed. Vic decided to let Tony British in on the heist and he gave him a carefully edited version of the plans. Tony British was delighted and he inspected the lorries closely to decide which one he was going to drive.

⤬ 16 ⤬

HIT THE ROAD

Vic drove a tank with the wagon made of oak. Prior to the custom job, it had the appearance of a supersized oak barrel on wheels. The exterior was now camouflaged with a thin sheet of metal to give it the effect of a regular oil tanker. It was even covered with a Shell logo to keep up appearances. The other lorries were in various shapes and sizes. The fleet was camouflaged to make it appear that each truck was on its own, hauling its payload, traversing the M6.

They were not associated in any way. Two were Tesco supermarket delivery lorries, and the other three were normal logistics lorries, all with different markings and logos. They would be very unlucky if one of them was to be pulled over by highway patrol on the lookout for stolen and illegal contraband. They were all legitimate looking vehicles, bearing the seals of some reputable companies. Thanks to Sam McDougal all the logos seemed authentic to the naked eye. The oil tanker seemed a little suspicious but Vic insisted that it would haul the most prized whisky in Scotland, the 'Grade A' pure undiluted stuff. He called it the 'Tear Jerker' because without a chaser one sip would make a grown man cry.

You could smell it from a mile. If the Old Bill pulled you over, they wouldn't bother to do the breathalyzer test. You would be nicked straightaway.

The 'Tear Jerker' was banned to the public. It had to be diluted and flavored before it could be sold. It was the base ingredient for most of the various types of expensive fancy name liquors on the shelves of five star hotels and exclusive social clubs. Some of the factory workers would shift and sell it to the local boozers who would then dilute it and make a killing. Vic himself participated in this trade, which was how he managed to prevent the pub from sinking further into the abyss of debt and in the hands of murderous creditors. Owing the Mussolini brothers was as bad as it could get, as far as Vic was concerned his life couldn't be any shittier than it was right now. He had no option but to go through with the heist and he was dead set on it. This was how he ended up on the road with Randy, his two stragglers Harry and Fred, Sam 'The Gun' MacDougal and Tony British who seemed to have gotten very close to Vic and JJ since the cock fight. He had long since returned Lucky to JJ and now they seemed to be best of friends. He must have spotted gold dust otherwise he would not waste his time sticking around. He would have been out and about looking for the next rewarding criminal activity.

⨯ 17 ⨯

WHISKY COUNTRY

The men entered 'Whisky Country' right on schedule. Their eager eyes scanned the area, building after building. All they saw were distilleries; hundreds of them lying quietly, as the white mist escaped into the atmosphere. White smoke meant that those distilleries were churning out the light stuff mass produced for retail. The men were looking for dark smoke which was very elusive, perhaps lost in the midst of the white smoke.

The brew the men were looking for could not be found on supermarket shelves. Some wine stores had the privilege of getting their hands on this brew and got away with charging exorbitant prices. The greedy bastards made over a thousand percent profit. They would acquire the goods cheaply from thieves on side roads, under basements and off the back of the lorries of dodgy delivery men. Though the wholesale prices were already profitable, the beautifully manufactured boxes which housed the brew were worth more than a bottle of the retail grade on the supermarket shelves. Vic himself was once involved in the trade; he reserved the brew for his high roller customers and for high stakes poker games where the players would spend any amount of cash to feel important. It was not really about the poker games but more about the battle of the biggest egos.

As the men continued on their brief sojourn in 'Whisky Country,' their nostrils started to capture the scent of pure over-proof whisky. The brew sat somewhere dark and quiet with its only disturbance being the intense, but cohesive chemical reaction that would produce its most delicate flavor. The first contact with the back of your throat would give you a jerk, and wake you up. Your eyes though now watering, you savor the taste of pure Scotland.

The place was dubbed 'Whisky Country'. All the buildings were exactly the same, with huge gates and high fences protecting the precious liquid that lay fermenting inside. The gates all had emblems that showed the seal and the established date of its distillery, and some were centuries old. Lining the yards were huge haulage lorries also boasting the name and seal of their respective brewer. Some had the proprietor's name written on the sides, evidently portraying the pride of the blend. The men joked that they would pick the names that they didn't like and rob those distilleries. However, they were not interested in the ones that lined the streets for those were handling the commercial part of the trade. Those distilleries made the stuff more palatable for the throats of those drinkers who couldn't handle the hard stuff.

Vic was interested in the over-proof, but those distilleries were anonymous and unmarked because, they only handled the raw material. You could get a million bottles of commercial grade whisky with just a few gallons. Hit one of those babies and Bob's your uncle. A tank-full alone could be worth tens of thousands of pounds. The robbers were interested in that stuff. There were also rumors that the 'Tear Jerker' was still being produced in large quantities in Scotland. Those rumors were what led Vic to choose Scotland as the mark for he could have robbed any brewery in or around London, but they were only small players. He needed to go to the source, to the land of real whisky. He knew that even a small amount could take care of all his financial problems. He went prepared with the tanker, carefully designed to handle one particular payload. He was the architect and McDougal was the contractor. They had restored and converted an old oil tanker that lay idle at the side of McDougal's garage. An old oil tanker that came in for repairs and was never retrieved. The outside still had its metallic shell, but the inside was carefully laid out with a thin layer of imitation oak, giving it a barrel like effect (not exactly the real thing) that could house the whisky for a few days. Then Vic would decide how he was going to store it long term for sale by the gallon, or if he was convincing enough he could get some exporter bloke to buy the whole lot.

McDougal had told Vic that if the 'Tear Jerker' was discovered, he would be satisfied with just a few gallons and that would be the only payment he needed for his contribution to the Great Whisky Heist. McDougal knew that if he had his own supply of 'Tear Jerker' he would never have to spend a penny on liquor for a very long time and that was his motivation. The thought of holding a glass with a splash of the pure undiluted stuff whetted his appetite. But, he had no idea how they were going to locate the distillery holding the treasure which he hunted.

The men were now approaching a denser part of 'Whisky Country'. The buildings were all the same. They couldn't tell whether they were distilleries or houses. One thing they were certain of was that almost everyone in whisky country took part in the trade. Extending from the distiller himself, the bloke who supplied the barley, who himself would have a small backyard production going on. Vic was interested in those guys. They were the ones who worked with small volumes, a 'mom and pop' operation, so to speak. They made it as pure as possible. That area of Glasgow seemed purposely built for whisky production. The setting was uniform, there were buildings for distillation and fermentation and then there were farms with thousands of acres of land lined with barley and other grains. People travelled from all over the country to visit these farms to get their hands on the brew. It was illegal for commercial sale because of its alcohol content, but business was booming on the black market and the players were some of the wealthiest blokes in the country.

⋊ 18 ⋉

THE MARK

The only indication that they were still in Whisky Country were the steel pipes on top of the roofs. The steam could be seen escaping, and then disappearing into the atmosphere. The smell of liquor was now stronger and McDougal salivated. He could taste the pure whisky by its smell; he swallowed then licked his lips ravenously.

The buildings were not as protected as the others on the other side of town; they looked like houses, meaning the brewers must have had their place of residence at the brewery. There were no huge lorries lining up awaiting their payload, only small utility vehicles parked in the yards. Whoever wanted to purchase some 'Tear Jerker' would have had to collect his merchandise in person. *Collection only...no home delivery.* The blokes producing the Tear Jerker were some of the most affluent men in Scotland. Vic knew that robbing any of these was not going to be an easy feat; they had very strong connections and would stop at nothing to show their strength and power. Even if Vic got away with the heist, he would have to be extra cunning to get rid of the merchandise without it being traced back to him. Some serious diluting and mixing would have to be done to disguise its origin. For this he would need James Johnston for his scientific mind and prowess in developing all sorts of concoctions, including but not limited to; poisons, moonshine and antidotes.

Vic spots his mark, a huge farm house at the end of a dirt road. It was isolated from the rest and was obviously designed to double as a brewery and living space. It almost looked desolate, but for its stately appearance. The grounds were well manicured, which gave the place its stately ambiance. It looked like old money and Fred and Harry were already at each other's throats arguing about the prospective loot inside awaiting the touch of their grubby little fingers. Randy reminded them why they were there; he told them that if they wanted to rob stately homes they could do it back in London. The two thieves could see Randy's point and immediately restrained themselves from strangling each other.

The place was starting to get dark and cloak like. Vic instructed Tony British to go and take a peak to see if anyone was home. Unlike the other breweries, there was no activity, no steam escaping with the scent of the hard stuff. No lights, but the protection system was fully engaged. The distant growls and grunts made Francis sound like a puppy. The men could not figure out if they were hearing pigs, bears or lions, but there was the strong notion that they were dealing with a diverse breed of animals. Beneath the heavy grunts and growls, they could detect the distinct sounds of Dobermans, Pit Bulls, and German Shepherds. All the big boys were accounted for.

Tony British was reluctant to go on the reconnaissance mission, but he had no choice because he was driving the smallest vehicle, so it would be easy for him to drive down the dirt road without the vehicle being heard or spotted. His job was to check for the presence of whisky and if they were lucky enough, he would bump into the mother-load. He was to first and foremost check if anyone was home. The size of his vehicle gave him some amount of comfort as he could make a quick escape if he was pounced upon by whatever creatures were making the ominously sounding grunts and growls. Vic placed Tony British mind at ease by referring to the fact that the place had all the hallmarks of a farm, which justified the strange sounds they were hearing. It was nevertheless, guaranteed that there were at least five dogs among the lot.

'It's an animal farm,' jeered Randy followed by his annoying laugh.

This notion gave Tony British no amount of comfort, as a matter of fact, his reluctance grew even stronger. Vic reminded him that the heist would be very rewarding and that he should consider himself lucky to be allowed to come along on the expedition. For this Tony British felt grateful, but he politely informed Vic that he would risk his life for money, but he would certainly not risk it for whisky. Sam McDougal who had been silent since they disembarked from their vehicles immediately volunteered when Tony British once again expressed his reluctance. McDougal's voice sounded distorted, his lips were dry and so was his throat. Vic immediately denied McDougal's request. He noticed that McDougal was thirsty and may not be able to contain himself if he found whisky and he once again laid down the no drink policy. The only drinking that would be allowed was to taste the merchandise to find out if it was top grade. The men confirmed their obedience, albeit reluctantly, especially the very thirsty McDougal.

Tony British now figured out that there was no way out for he was the owner of the vehicle that was best poised to carry out the reconnaissance with minimal chance of being noticed. The men watched as the vehicle disappeared from sight. The only indication that the vehicle was there were the lights which gave it a hovering appearance.

⊰ 19 ⊱

THE RECONNAISSANCE MISSION

T_ony British now made his way_ down the graveled road leading to the farmhouse. He hated dogs and now he had no choice but to go face his fears. The vehicle coasted silently, and he stopped a short distance from the gate and then decided to go on foot for the remainder of the journey. As he approached the gate, his eyes remained peeled as he surveyed the yard. He was looking out for anything with teeth or fangs. The sounds that he had heard from the road had ceased and that made him concerned.

He was conveniently clad in dark clothing, so he blended in with the darkness. The place appeared lifeless, no humans or animals were in sight, but there was a distinct smell. It was an unfamiliar smell, but he sensed it must be something precious. He circled the perimeter of the house and as he approached the back he saw what they were looking for, black smoke. Jackpot! It was dark and he was excited. The smoke could not be seen from the road due to the design of the ventilation system. The pipes were not protruding upwards, they were facing outwards. When the smoke was finally lifted in the atmosphere it would have done so a far distance from the house. One would have to be nearby to be convinced that the smoke was not just vapor rising from the earth.

Tony British climbed the fence to make a more detailed inspection of the premises. He made his way over to the farmhouse where he saw a large jumble of shiny metal pipes protruding from the building, then stretching downwards to disappear into the ground. He followed his line of vision which led him into the fields. He couldn't believe what he was seeing; black smoke was coming out of the earth. His heart skipped a beat and he turned to run in the direction from whence he came, but he halted abruptly when he heard Randy's disturbing laughter.

The other men had followed shortly behind him and was now taking the piss seeing him shudder in fright.

He said, 'You think this is bloody funny? If I was McDougal's age, I would have probably had a heart attack!'

The men laughed even harder after Tony British spoke and they only stopped when they noticed that he was becoming infuriated.

⋊ 20 ⋉

THE REUNION

The six men surveyed the premises. Vic was in deep thought. 'The place seemed to be working but no living souls at the controls. Brewing was certainly taking place; the smoke had to be released somewhere and if one was knowledgeable about whisky distillation then one could tell the grade of whisky just by looking at the smoke. Whoever owned the property certainly spent a lot of money to disguise his activities; for the untrained eyes would certainly not have connected the smoke to the building.' Vic inspected the smoke more closely and noticed that it was mixed. He could see white smoke mingling with the black. 'It was a perfect disguise.' 'One could not easily tell what blend is being made here,' He said out loud, unconsciously.

'You are absolutely right Victor, one could not tell, but you could, my drunkard of a son-in-law.' said a calm familiar sounding voice.

Vic was startled. 'What the...John Glass, I didn't know this was your place or else I wouldn't have.' Vic said staring fearfully at the nozzle of the hunting rifle which Glass held in his hands.

'But you did do that Victor; you always take what is

not yours to take. You can't help yourself, you are a petty criminal always looking for the next score. Look at your men! They are a disgrace. That old geezer seems to be falling over himself and those two idiots over there, acting fidgety, are making me feel agitated, and when I feel agitated my fingers twitch, so you don't want me holding a bloody shooter pointed at you when I feel agitated, so tell them to stop bloody fidgeting!' The calm voice now transformed into rage.

He then took out a small shiny instrument from his top jacket pocket and blew into it. As if a volcano had erupted and Armageddon was at hand, the menacing sounds returned and they were close. The men stood frozen in place as the canine titans stealthily assumed a battle like formation before them. Each man was marked and none dared twitched. An evil smile appeared on Glass's face and Vic noticed that he was pleased with the situation. It was all a trap, a setup, Vic could tell. All the angles went through his mind. The connection that provided the Intel must have been watching him very closely and her name was clear as day in his mind. He should have known everything was just too dandy. She was just a pawn sent to confuse his mind with passion, which blinded his eyes to the events that delivered him to the courtyard of the man that longed to judge him for the death of his daughter and grandsons.

'I know what you are thinking Victor, but no, well yes, in a sense, but not directly' said Glass.

Detective Dawson made his presence known by clearing his throat. He had been standing by the side of the farm house listening to Glass with an amused look on his face.

'This here is Detective Dawson. I don't believe you met him, he is her partner. They both work for me, but the funny thing is, neither of them knows.' said Glass looking at Dawson.

Detective Dawson looked back with a sense of pride.

'He did his job, he brought you to me. Sorry Detective.'

Before the Detective could even blink, a single shot from the rifle pierced his heart.

'I don't like complications Vic,' said a remorseless Glass.

The men had time to be astonished and Tony British's eyes were looking for a safe haven.

'I don't like thieves such as you all, I will use you, but I find you most despicable. Tonight Victor you are going to pay your debt and your accomplices over there are going to give you a helping hand. You are all going to help me rob my enemies. What you can't take, you will contaminate. I want to put them out of business permanently.' He looked closely at each man and then his attention returned to Vic and he said, 'I wish we could have all gathered under friendlier circumstances. I could have told you a story that would blow your minds and it is because you don't know the story, that's why you are in this predicament. I could easily feed you to my dogs, but I find that you can be useful to me. If you do a great job, then maybe I won't feed you to the dogs and perhaps I will tell you the story and you all will be rich.'

With the dogs still holding their position, the men listened intently, but they dared not move. One moment Glass was in rage next thing they knew he was putting forth a proposition that they could not refuse. He was now just an innocent Scottish land owner getting robbed. He was not involved in the legitimate whisky trade. He gave it up a long time ago. He was just a barley farmer for all his neighbors knew. Of course he was expected to do a little brewing even for personal consumption; after all he was a resident of Whisky Country, albeit a very low key one. What the neighbors did not know was that he was producing a blend with an alcoholic content a hundred times stronger than what they were producing. He was not producing on a large scale, but it could be concentrated resulting in a volume to match any of the large distilleries.

'What about the Detective?' Vic enquired.

'Don't worry about that. Just say that he will be packaged, shipped and left at sea,' replied Glass.

Glass immediately changed the subject. 'You see gentlemen, Whisky Country has great wealth. The top families around here have been brewing for centuries. These families control eighty percent of the whisky brewing business in Scotland, but me, I am just a farmer, a small link on the supply chain. But the brewers, they are the fat cats.'

'Ok, let me get this straight, you want us to rob these breweries for you?' Randy interjected.

Everybody including Glass turned to look at Randy. They were all surprised that he was brave enough to speak, but the dogs were well trained, they would not attack unless commanded by their master.

'Give a round of applause to the genius over there. Victor, I thought all your men were dumb,' said Glass in a sarcastic tone.

Vic could not help but laugh, he was amused at the way Glass said it.

'You see gentlemen, I am the only producer of the 'Tear Jerker,' said Glass with a pride filled tone. 'Ok, let me give you a little taste of the story I mentioned. You see, everyone in Scotland thinks the 'Tear Jerker' is a myth because they have never seen or tasted it. I never sold it in Scotland. I exported it to America and business was booming in their era of prohibition. My associates and I used to ship it under the guise of ethanol. My exporter contact in London was highly respected and had connections the world over, so his vessels were never scrutinized. We did it for years, but somebody snitched and our operation was halted because the Scottish authorities destroyed the equipment and they were not easy to replace, so we gave it up. This is why you only know me as a hardworking farmer. It took me years to replace the equipment, but I did and I started distilling the beautiful stuff a few years back. The first batch is now ready for shipping and my new connection in London is awaiting delivery. It will be just like the old days.'

The men listened intently and Glass noticed that they wanted more, but he did not oblige them.

'You know Glass, what I don't understand is why you didn't come to me all these years. With your guidance I wouldn't have resorted to this and you know that I could sell anything to anyone,' said Vic.

'That was a part of the long-term plan, you would have been inducted into our society, but you made some grave mistakes. You got drunk and killed my family. You acquired The Refuge by shady means. You became exposed and that's not a good thing for us. You became a common criminal who wouldn't know how to handle the vast wealth that we would have given to you. But you owe me, you always did, and now you and your cohorts will do exactly as I say,' responded Glass.

⊰ **21** ⊱

THE TOUR

Glass *blew into the silent* whistle and the dogs disappeared as quickly as they had arrived. He instructed the men to bring the lorries around the back, so they would be out of sight. His neighbors knew that he did not own so many vehicles and if they saw them, it would arouse suspicion, especially when they discovered that they had been robbed on the next visit to their distilleries.

Glass figured that since it was Saturday night, the brewers wouldn't discover the heist until Monday. So that gave them several hours to do the job. The only obstacles that they would have to contend with were the security guards and he knew exactly how to deal with them.

The men returned from hiding the vehicles and he instructed them to follow him into the house. He purposely told them not to touch anything.

'I know you are petty criminals, but I want you to appreciate the fact that you will be embarking on the biggest job of your careers, so keep your grubby hands off my antiques. As a matter of fact keep your eyes off them, just focus in the direction you are walking,' said Glass.

The men obeyed and they followed him to an elevator.

They entered and noticed that the only direction was down. The journey must have lasted for a few minutes and a look of curiosity was etched across their faces.

'Gentlemen, you are literally going back in time, this place was constructed many centuries ago by my ancestors who opposed the king at the time, they were tired of being burnt out, so they went underground and this became their refuge and it is now mine. It is because of this place why my bloodline escaped complete annihilation, but even in these modern times we are still being attacked. It has changed from sabotage to unfair competition in business,' responded Glass to their unasked questions.

He continued, 'The revenge that I am going to dish out on my enemies has been a long time coming. The bloodline of the ancient kings and their court still exists today and they still control Scotland. We were almost reduced to poverty and I am the last of the Glass clan standing. That's why I can never forgive you Vic; you killed my grandsons and the heirs to my estate. You did in one night what the enemies of my family tried to do over many centuries. You destroyed my bloodline!'

The elevator reached its destination and Glass like a true host allowed the men to exit first. The men looked astonished as they entered a cavernous lair. The space was vast and something told them that they were only in the foyer. If an intruder managed to find the elevator and discovered the cavern, he might think that he has just entered an old mine shaft. They took their eyes off Glass as they surveyed the cavern; however, their curiosity was interrupted by the sound of a huge door opening. As they turned to face the direction of the sound, they saw a large concrete slab rotating on an axis. They also discovered that Glass was no longer with them. McDougal was the first to follow for he was anxious to find out what awaited them on the other side. The other men followed swiftly behind for they too wanted some of that which McDougal was in pursuit.

On the other side of the concrete door, they were not prepared for what they were about to see. The place was magnificent, it was a pity such beauty and splendor was locked away from sight. They saw a number of paintings that were carefully hung up in the perfect place. The Persian rugs with their beautiful color patterns adorned the floor. Statues of Roman Emperors lined a walkway leading to what looked like a golden throne. Another section held a wide array of weapons that seemed to come from every era. The men could not identify some of the modern looking weapons, which seemed to have been made from space age technology. There were other sections that looked like vaults and it did not take a strong imagination to assume what lay inside them. The things they saw could easily fill any of the large museums in London. The place was obviously not a storage facility or an old basement where antiques go to die, but rather a living space that was fit for a king. It felt like a lair where evil men seek cover from the prying eyes of the public to perfect their sinister plots.

Glass looked at the men while they drool over his possessions. He sensed that they were confused, wishing they could question out loud everything they were seeing. They knew better than to ask questions for no answers would be given to them tonight. The reunion with Vic wasn't exactly friendly, he and his cohorts knew that they were not in a position to ask questions, so they just stood there looking gob-smacked. Glass was pleased that they were astounded by his possessions maybe he could use this show of power and achievement as a tool to control them.

Vic was lost in thought, Randy had a soundless grin

on his face, Tony British was looking for a way out, Harry and Fred were still eyeballing the antiques and McDougal was thirsty. He was eyeing the half bottle of whisky lying patiently on a desk located in arm's reach. The moment he entered the room the first thing he saw was a WW1 Browning machine gun sitting on a huge oak mantel piece and then the bottle of whisky. He wondered if they both came from the same era. Each time he looked at a piece of antique his eyes would return to the bottle. Glass saw that he was in dire need of a drink and offered him one.

McDougal reached for the bottle but he was cut off by Vic who grabbed his hand and said, 'McDougal, remember we have a no drink policy until the job is done, I am sure everybody is dying for a drink, so control your bloody self!'

Glass interjected and said, 'I am in charge now and if I say he can have a drink he is going to have a drink, now what will it be McDougal, I will join you. I have a vast collection of vintage whisky.'

McDougal's eyes lit up when he heard the words 'collection', 'vintage' and 'whisky' all in the same sentence. Somehow, the word yes could not pass his scorched lips, so he nodded to show his acceptance.

Then Glass said, 'As a matter of fact, we are all going to have a drink and quite frankly this offer cannot be refused. I caught you trying to steal from me, but because of the love for my daughter I have invited you in as guests. Would you dare refuse me Victor?'

Vic with a blocked throat answered and said, 'Ok Glass, we will have one drink. We are keen on hearing what you want us to do. I am deeply sorry for what happened to Angie and the boys and God knows I have been through living hell for it. As you know I was sent to Pentonville for several years then to Bedlam. I yield to you for you have yet to punish me personally and I am willing to do anything you ask of me. I know it won't be enough to heal the wounds of my folly, but I hope it will be a show of my acknowledgment that I committed an unforgiveable act.'

Glass was fuming at the fact that Vic dared to mention the names of his daughter and grandsons. He did not respond and his silence made the men nervous. He then interrupted the silence, 'Let us go have that drink. Come with me to my drawing room.'

With that said, the men formed a single file and Glass led them down the aisle towards the throne. Upon reaching the throne, he reached into his pocket and took out a remote control. He pressed it and the throne began to regress.

McDougal somehow managed to release a few words from his dry mouth 'This place is full of tricks and treats.'

Glass looked at McDougal with a raised eyebrow and said, 'Yes, my old friend and if you were truly clever, then you would have been rich as well. But instead you decided to be an educated fool and you turned out to be nothing but an old tramp and a vagrant. A total bloody waste of space you are. I bet you are still trying to build back up that broken down garage of yours. You are all lucky the Italians haven't decided to kill you yet. You must be worth something to them.'

Vic eyes became less reflective and Glass noticed. He said, 'Tell me Vic, did they send you here to rob me? For it would certainly be a coincidence that my enemies' friends who are your enemies sent you here to rob me. I see you fellows are caught up in a conundrum. Hmmm, I wonder how you are going to work your way out of this one Victor.'

After what seemed like an eternity, the throne finally reached its destination. The men looked on in amazement as Glass disappeared down a stairway.

'What the hell is this place?' asked Tony British.

Randy answered, 'And how exactly are we to know that? Let us just follow the bloke and see where he leads us. Nothing from here on out will surprise me. This guy is freaking James Bond. I have seen caverns, trap doors, gadgets, and the whole lot.'

He gave out a tuned down version of his annoying laughter and proceeded to lead the way to Glass's intra-terrestrial abode. The other men followed and discovered that the stairway led to another elevator.

Glass was waiting with a broad grin on his face. He said, 'I trust by now you have all realized that you are at a place where very few men had the privilege to enter. Just don't get any fancy ideas and you all will be handsomely rewarded. From here on out I will do all the thinking.'

≍ **22** ≍

THE PLOT

Glass instructed the men to enter the elevator and they filed in obediently. Inside they noticed that this elevator could travel in both directions, but again they were going down. When they reached their destination, they saw what appeared to be a den kit out with leather chairs and oak furniture. They also noticed a room with loads of television monitors and top class surveillance equipment. They all looked at each other knowingly. Glass must have seen them a mile away and he had the element of surprise. Showing on some of the screens were what looked like distilleries, but they did not see any large distilleries near the property, so they figured that he must be staking out some of the breweries they had passed on the other side of Whisky Country.

'This way Gentlemen,' Glass instructed.

The men entered an oval room with a large round table and black leather chairs, a large throne like chair stood out and it didn't take a stretch of the imagination to figure out whose seating place it was.

'Have a seat while I go fetch a bottle of whisky,' said Glass as he exited the room.

The men looked at each other with a sense of

importance, they were sitting in a boardroom eager to hear Glass's plans, but none of them said a word as they were keener on hearing rather than speaking.

Glass returned carrying a tray with a very beautifully shaped bottle and some stylish tumblers and he had what appeared to be a large map folded under his right arm.

He said, 'Ok let us have that drink. Who will be the first to have a swig of this precious brew?'

McDougal answered and said, 'You are too kind, but I think I will have a drink of water instead. Vic was right, we need to keep a clear head at least after we are done with whatever you want us to do.'

Glass responded, 'Ah, Samuel don't you trust me? Or should I say Sam 'The Gun McDougal'. Why are you looking surprised Sam? After all that I have said earlier you still don't recognize me. Well, allow me to refresh your memory.' He then poured himself a glass and emptied the contents down his throat. Harry and Fred now assumed that the brew was safe to drink commandeered the bottle and a couple glasses. They too knocked off their whisky just as quickly as Glass did, and poured a second round, but this time they decided to nurse their glasses.

Vic, Randy and Tony British seemed unconcerned about the whisky; they were more interested in hearing what Glass was about to say about knowing McDougal. They straightened up in their seats and cocked their ears in anticipation of his words.

He said, 'We don't have a lot of time, but I think it is prudent that we clear the air. Yes, I know McDougal and it is such a pity he hasn't recognized me. Mind you, I was a very handsome young chap. Not the stressed out droopy eyed person you are staring at now, but I was a real catch with the ladies back in the old days. We became very wealthy at a young age my best mate and I who I don't care to mention by name. How did we do it? You might ask! We were smart; we were sailors in the royal navy before we became merchants. We knew the sea and we sailed upon it for the better part of our young lives, but we made damn good use of it. You see, it was the era of prohibition in the United States and we milked it. We would set up accounts with some of the meanest mobsters in Chicago and New York. What we did was to set up a bank account for a bogus glass bottle factory called Glasgow's Glass. Our customers would set up bogus companies that had use for the glass bottles and glassware we were supposedly manufacturing. Our customers received their orders indeed, but the bottles were certainly not empty. We were very careful to hide our faces from the mobsters and they did not know our names. All they had was an account number and the coordinates to the drop points at sea. It was minimum risk for us and maximum risk for them. All we had to do was get the merchandise on the ship. Even if the payload was discovered, untrained nostrils would not be able to tell if it was whisky or ethanol. We would make the drop off at certain points at sea and our job was done. The bootleggers would risk sharks and coast guards to retrieve their goods and many were not successful. Sometimes the plan would get botched by them arriving at the spot too early and get themselves in shootouts with our ship because they were out there floating idly and looking suspicious. We would have already received payment, so no loss to us, but we were stuck with the whisky. We would then barter with the tradesmen at the ports which we would stop at to collect supplies from the natives. We weren't interested in their currency only gold and artifacts and we discovered that they had a lot of gold and even diamonds. We started doing it full time when we realized that the merchant business was more lucrative and healthier than trading with the mobsters. Furthermore, gold was king back then and as you all know it still is. Most of what you see down here is things that we acquired from our many voyages across the world trading the good old Scottish whisky. The things we have seen and done, my mate and me, you would not believe. Our operation was foiled and we were dishonorably discharged from the navy, but that was a blessing because we were now free to do what we wanted and the world became our oyster. So, we got ourselves a ship and became full time merchants. We traded everything from a pin to an anchor and the whisky was married to them all.' Glass took a deep breath, and then he looked around the table, each man getting five seconds of his piercing eyes.

His eyes caught McDougal's last and he smiled at him. He continued his story, 'How does McDougal come into the picture you might ask? Well, McDougal over there was a chemist along with his mate James Johnston; they were very good, but McDougal had a drinking problem which distorted his judgment. You only know him as a mechanic and if you are a dim wit then you would believe that he was a SAS sniper. The only shooting range he has ever been to was at the skeet club. Though, I must say that he was very good at shooting down those clay pigeons.'

Glass laughed and so did Randy. Vic shot him a shut your glob look and his annoying laughter ceased.

Glass continued, 'He and Johnston was responsible for disguising the 'Tear Jerker' as ethanol, but he was clumsy, which led the authorities to discover our operation and it was shut down. As a result we lost millions of pounds worth of liquor, and our trading route with our United States allies was completely shut down. All this happened due to the loosening of his tongue after he had a few drinks.'

McDougal had a reminiscent look on his face and he sunk deep in his seat. He said, 'I will have that drink now. That was a very long time ago and I admit I was very young and foolish back then.'

'I forgive you. It was a very long time ago indeed and the authorities never did figure out who the masterminds were. They thought we were just handlers, small timers. The funny thing was that they thought we were being paid to load the crates unto the ship,' said Glass while he filled McDougal's glass.

'Thank you,' said McDougal.

Glass looked at him and said, 'I must commend you on the fact that you did not give us away during the trial. Even though we were furious at you for messing up our operation, in time we realized that you actually did us a favor and I no longer wanted to choke the life out of you.'

He paused for a moment in thought and stared at Vic and said, 'You see there are certain things I am willing to forget, but there are some things that are simply unforgettable.'

Vic swallowed some saliva and filled a glass with shaking hands. He spilled some of the whisky on the oak table and Glass let out a grunt, but did not say a word. Randy the only remaining man yet to partake in the whisky reached for a glass and poured his drink with equally shaky hands.

Glass said, 'Ok, now seeing that most things are out in the open and I have shocked you all into having a drink let me now plan your heist for you. Forget about whatever plan Victor and McDougal made. I don't know what it was, but I am sure it would have been very foolish. You have already been caught before you had a chance to even look at what you travelled hundreds of miles to steal.'

The men felt embarrassed that their plot was foiled

before it even got started.

'Now listen up,' said Glass as he rolled out a large map of Scotland on the table. 'Tonight we are going to pull off the greatest whisky heist in history and we are going to do it all in one night.'

He paused and looked at them curiously, wondering if he should give them another history lesson. Maybe they should know, he thought. Then they would have a clearer understanding of the necessity of this undertaking. '*Ok, I will tell them.*' He stepped away from the table and put both his hands behind his back. He paced around the table and came to a stop at the throne. He gasped and sat down with a look of pain and hatred in his eyes. He said, 'Gentlemen, I know you are not in a position to question the reasons for my actions, but I think you ought to know the background to what I am going to make you do tonight. You see, Scotland is a very old country. In the beginning it was ruled by clans, and then out of the clans kings were crowned and they appointed lords to run the affairs of different areas of the land. These lords became wealthy and powerful and the domain for which they used to oversee assumed their names and this has remained to date. Just take a look at the map before you. The names of all those places you see were named after the lords and their wealth and influence still exists to this day. Their bloodlines still control Scotland; they own the deeds to all the cities. They also have an iron grip on the Scottish whisky trade for they owned the largest distilleries.'

The men seemed very interested to hear more and Glass would oblige them, but first he had some questions to ask. 'So, tell me Vic, what exactly was your plan? I am keen to hear it; maybe there is a one in a million chance that it is similar to mine. Maybe you are smarter than I thought, after all your plan got you this far. Who knows, if you had targeted another property probably you would have been successful, but you chose the wrong place and as a result you came up dry. Go on then, please do tell.'

Vic looked at Glass and Glass looked back in anticipation for the answer to his question. Vic wondered if he should tell him plan B or just admit that he was in desperate pursuit of the 'Tear Jerker' and that he did not exactly have a target. He knew what he was looking for, but he wasn't sure if he would find it. He found what he was looking for, but was not expecting the Glass surprise. Half the men in the room did not know the real reason why he was in Scotland on the hunt for the best whisky to steal. They knew he had financial problems and that it was all about the money. He was not sure if he should disclose the fact that they have travelled hundreds of miles just to rescue a huge over fed pit bull. He suspected that Glass was winding him up because if he was expecting them then he must have known everything. He had to come straight or else Glass was sure to call him out as a liar and that would not make him look good in the eyes of his cohorts.

Glass saw that Vic was lost in thought and decided to add some fuel to the fire. He said, 'Go on Victor, and tell your men the real reason why they are here. I am sure they will understand, after all whisky and money is in it for them. They have nothing to lose, but respect for you. However, they came this far and I am sure they want to get paid and as such they will see the job through.'

Tony British interjected and said, 'Tell us Vic, why exactly are we here? I deserve to know, you sent me on the reconnaissance mission and I could have been mauled by dogs or worse yet, I could have been shot like poor old Detective Dawson.'

Vic did not acknowledge Tony British's words. Instead, he stared squarely at Glass and said, 'Go on Glass, you seem to have your ears to the ground, so you tell them the reason why we are here.'

Glass responded and said, 'This is not a game Victor, I asked you a question and I expect you to answer it truthfully. We need everything in the open. After all, we are all friends here. Am I correct in saying so gentlemen?'

The men looked at each other and then they looked at Glass and nodded in agreement.

McDougal had remained silent and he did not give a verbal or a physical response to Glass's question. He was deep in thought trying to remember the time in the navy that Glass mentioned earlier. He now remembered Glass and his mate clearly and then he remembered the colt he had concealed in his coat pocket. With an uncontrolled reflexive action, he moved his right hand to his pocket to gently massage the gun with his fingers. He then removed his hand quickly and his eyes met those of Glass. Glass got up from his throne and took up position behind it for what he saw in McDougal's eyes indicated that he was ready to pounce at any second. Glass pushed a button and the men could hear metals maneuvering until suddenly to their surprise a Gatling gun was seated before them where Glass had sat. The men now had fear in their eyes and they were confused about the sudden change in Glass. Even more confusing was the sight of the big gun sitting before them with Glass holding a remote control firmly in his hand. 'Are you men armed?' he asked firmly.

The men responded with a resounding no and then looked around the table to see if any of their colleagues were lying. McDougal's 'no' sounded a bit dodgy. It sounded more like a clearing of the throat rather than a clear and confident 'no'. He now seemed uneasy with all the eyes in the room focused on him. Glass punched a command into the remote control and the nozzle of the Gatling gun was now also focused on him.

Vic rushed to McDougal's defense verbally and said, 'Ok, we have some irons, but they are in one of the lorries. I am confident in saying that no man here is armed.'

Glass repeated the statement a second time, but this time it sounded like a question rather than a statement.

McDougal threw up is arms and said, 'Ok, I have a colt concealed in my top left jacket pocket.'

The nozzle of the gun was still pointed towards him. The other men looked at McDougal wondering what his next words would be. They were clear and unruffled. He said, 'I am going to reach in slowly and remove the pistol, then I am going to place it on the table.'

Glass without blinking said, 'Ok, go on, but do it slowly and remove the bullets after which I want you to slide the gun across the table to me. Make no mistakes McDougal, I will shoot you.'

'Ok, take it easy,' responded McDougal.

He then reached into his pocket and removed what looked like a gun. It was hard to tell exactly what it was for it seemed to have armored itself with a huge layer of rust. Everyone laughed including Glass at the contraption McDougal removed from his coat pocket.

Glass said, 'Really! Ok, now remove the bullets and slide it over to me.'

McDougal did what he was told, and with shaking hands he emptied the barrel and sent the gun sailing across the huge table.

Glass showed his powerful reflexive muscles and caught the pistol just before it reached the end of the table. He took it up and inspected it carefully. He then looked up at McDougal and smiled. He said, 'This barrel is as clean as a whistle. You could have done plenty damage with this thing. You are no fool, are you McDougal? You give the impression that you are an eccentric old man, but you are very clever aren't you? Now I am feeling very paranoid. Did you come here to kill me? Vic over there, seemed very surprised to see me, but you, you acted like you didn't know me. That tells me you were expecting this encounter and you made certain you were prepared. What you didn't know my dear old friend is that I have always been ten steps ahead and you will soon discover that patience is the most important virtue a man could ever possess.'

McDougal looked at him, but did not give an answer to any of his questions.

Glass then looked at Vic and said, 'McDougal has been using you all along. He hitched a ride thinking that he could come up here, get his revenge and be back in London for Sunday tea. One thing you should know, his loyalty is to Scotland and it will always be so. Some years after he gave up our operation to the authorities, I discovered that he was working for my enemies all along and I wasn't the only one trading whisky on the high seas. He sold our formula to the whisky producing families. They were instrumental in shutting us down and then they took over.'

'Lies, bloody lies,' McDougal shouted bravely.

Glass ignored him and continued to speak, 'When the prohibition laws were repealed, they were already in a position to go legit, while my mate and I scampered from shore to shore trying to evade the law who were now actually working for the big whisky companies to stamp out the bootleggers. We made a lot of money, but had to remain low key and as such our names were unknown while the other families got cities and streets named after them just like in the old days when my ancestors were alive. Tonight it all ends, I am going to destroy them and if I cannot then we will at least put a large dent in their operation. As I said before, we will take what the lorries can hold then we are going to contaminate every last barrel of whisky that remains. They will not know what hit them and it will take years for them to supply the market with aged whisky again.'

Glass paused for a moment to catch his breath and Vic used the opportunity to throw in his two pence. He said, 'That will no doubt cripple the Scottish economy as whisky is their main export.'

Glass looked at Vic sternly and said, 'That's exactly the intention. There are powers at work here that you cannot begin to understand, so don't ask for the reasons or the rationale behind my pending actions.'

He looked around the room and noticed Randy with his hand held up high like a little schoolboy eager to ask his question. 'What is it?' shouted Glass.

'I have the notion that you won't be coming along. Instead you are just going to sit back and watch us do the job on your little monitors.' responded Randy.

Vic shot him the shut your glob look again, but Randy ignored it. Instead, as if bravery was now his best friend, he looked Glass square in the eyes and said, 'You have this all planned out haven't you? You set it all up every intricate detail; I am even starting to suspect that you may have had some arrangements with Big Mike.'

Glass smiled at him devilishly, while the other men looked on in astonishment at Randy who had a look of anticipated victory on his face. The timid little boy had asked his question and now eagerly awaits the answer.

Vic saw an opening and decided to give Randy some support. He cleared his throat to ensure that his speech would be firm and coherent. He looked at Glass and said, 'Randy's notion sounds plausible and I am led to believe that you may also have a hand in Francis' disappearance.'

Upon hearing those words McDougal shot Glass an evil glance and then settled back down into the abyss of his guilt.

As if the Gatling gun was not present, Vic continued to explore his new found bravery. He said, 'You lured me here with one thing on your mind. Revenge! And you want it to be done with pawns while you the master player set the moves and then sit back and watch the game. My desperation caused my judgment to become cloudy and my sense of awareness waned. To tell you the truth Glass, I don't know how I lasted this long. I have to be dodging every criminal in East London. My life since Angie died has been a total suicide for I have died so many times and yet still I remain breathing, living, enjoying all the amenities of life, but the place which houses my soul remains empty.'

Glass upon hearing the profound words that exited Vic's mouth smiled and looked at him in admiration of his ability to string a set of words so eloquently.

He said, 'I hear you Victor, I have visited that place and to tell you the truth men like us don't belong there. We must pick ourselves up and move on conquering our fears as we pursue wealth and power. I must admit, your bravery is admirable, you were stone broke and you long suffered for many years, but you thought and you planned your way out of the doldrums of poverty. And here you are right now sitting in front of me with your cards all played out while your men look on in bewilderment and defeat. I won't kill you Vic, after all you are family and you know what that means don't you? We look out for each other and it pains me to say this but you are the closest thing to a family I have left. I have associates that are like family to me, but you are the closest thing I have to my bloodline my daughter gave birth to your seed.'

Vic looked at Glass with glossy eyes has he remembered his family and the happy times they spent together. Glass never liked him and he was always conscious of that fact, so he would not be fooled by his words. He was going to play it out even though he was yet to figure out Glass' true intentions.

Glass interrupted Vic's thoughts and said, 'Enough of this, let me get down to the 'intricate' details as Randy studiously stated.' He then punched a command into the remote control and the Gatling gun disappeared. The men were able to now breathe more freely, but before they could relax they heard a mechanical movement and wondered what was next to pop out.

At that point Glass folded the large map of Glasgow which he had rolled out on the table. He turned his attention to the north side of the room where the ominous sound was coming from. He then smiled and said, 'Randy is correct, I won't be partaking in the heist physically. I am going to sit in the comfort of my den and monitor it. I will be watching your every move, so don't you get any smart ideas. Now, turn your attention to the screen and tell me what you notice about the map of Scotland and the cities therein.'

The men responded with a collective 'Hmmm...err.'

Glass interrupted their pondering and said, 'Ok tell me what you notice about the word Glasgow?

Again the men were in a stupor, however Randy managed to snap out of it and he said, 'I know! The first three letters are part of your surname and all the major cities and towns in Scotland bear the surname of people.'

Glass with a smile on his face turned to Randy and said, 'You continue to surprise me and I am starting to think that you are the smartest out of the lot. You are correct; the names that you see on the map are that of wealthy explorers, military men and colonizers who helped to enrich the crown. My family was one of the most powerful in Scotland. The other families got cities and towns named after them including Edinburgh,

Dumbarton, Dundee, Stirling, Paisley, Aberdeen and Inverness, to name a few. After the fall of my family due to the traitors within our midst our wealth began to decline and we had to sell a lot of land. What wasn't sold was stolen by our enemies who surrounded us like vultures waiting to feed on the dying carcass. They started to carve up sections of Glasgow for themselves and attached their names to them. You passed them on your way to me, the three that upset me the most are Paisley, Dumbarton and Kilbride. The records of my ancestors showed that they took over the land by force. We had no army to protect our domain and we were cornered in. Eventually they managed to wipe us out and this property is all that remained. I don't know if it is out of sympathy for us why they kept the name Glasgow, but I am happy they did for even though I only own this small parcel of land, I am proud to know that one of the greatest cities in Scotland still bears my family name and crest.'

McDougal upon hearing the story looked on the screen with deep interest. He now figured out what Glass was planning. He was planning revenge to right the wrongs of many centuries ago. He decided to ask a question. He said, 'Tell me Glass, how are you going to take your revenge on all the towns bearing the names of these families?'

Glass looked at McDougal in annoyance and said, 'Tell me my fellow countryman, from which family do you hail? I am sure you are from peasant stock for I don't see any cities or towns in Scotland bearing the name McDougal. So, I don't think you would understand the fire that burnt in my heart. I am restless and I will not die before I get my revenge.'

McDougal said, 'My family too was hurt by the land grabs, which is why I ended up in England. We had to flee for we did not have the power and wealth to defend our domain as your family did. I haven't been back to my beloved Scotland since I was a boy, so I can relate to your intentions. Revenge would have been my consoler also if I knew who the perpetrators were. It happened within this century and I cannot find any records of the event. Therefore, I am intrigued that you know your enemies, but I must inquire. How do you know exactly who the descendants are? I am sure that the names have changed from generation to generation through marriage, infidelity and deed polls.'

He responded, 'That is a very good question McDougal and the answer is simple. I followed the symbols. By this I mean the emblems and the crests. These never change and they are in the public domain for all to research and find. It took me a while to discover this method of finding my enemies, but I was successful.'

McDougal was keen on hearing more for maybe he could find the descendants of his family's enemies.

Glass continued, 'I am not a violent man, so I couldn't bring myself to kill anyone. I could have, but then the voice of reason spoke and told me that these descendants may not know anything of their ancestor's misdeeds, so it was not fair to harm them, so I decided to harm their enterprise. The largest distilleries in whisky country are owned by them. Bring your attention back to the screen and study the emblems closely for they are the targets. We are going to put them completely out of business.'

The men looked at the screen and noticed that some of the emblems looked familiar. They recalled seeing some of them on their way in and others they have seen on pubs back in London.

Glass saw the knowing expressions on the men faces and he looked at Vic and said, 'Yes Victor, some of these emblems may look very familiar to you for they are the trademark of your competitors. They have a choke hold on the whisky trade by controlling both the wholesale and the retail. They own the pubs and these pubs have an endless supply of brew while you struggle to keep your customers throats wet. Why do you think they lasted so long? Your pub was also a beneficiary of this sneaky trade for the past owners had their supply straight from the source. My family used to ensure that The Refuge always had a constant supply of fire water. It used to serve the best Scottish whisky and it used to be the most popular. It was the first to have direct links to the Scottish brewers, however, the others figured it out and started doing the same thing and the competition became fierce and even resulted in a lot of bloodshed. They changed the names of the pubs just as you did, but the emblems remained intact. I am sure you didn't even take the time to figure out what the emblem on your pub meant for you would have figured out the connection, but you were too busy being dodgy and as such you missed the big picture. It is all about symbols my friend and if you are not clued up then you will not see that everything in this world is linked to lineage, money and power. I hope you all have been listening keenly for all that I have told you are some hidden secrets that the layman is not privy to.'

He pressed the remote control and three large buildings popped up on the screen. He said, 'These distilleries are the ones we are going to rob tonight. They bear the crest of Paisley, Dumbarton and Kilbride. Conveniently for us, they are in close proximity to each other and I have had them under surveillance for over a decade waiting for the opportune moment to strike. I was too liberal with my plans and I forgot that traitors still existed. If I had launched an attack then it would be easily traced back to me, so instead I waited until the traitors disappeared and I too went underground. Nobody knows that I am here. They know that my farm is active, but they think I am in America. I stocked up with supplies and I bunkered in perfecting my plans. I must say it was not easy getting you here for it had to be perfect and without a trace. So you see gentlemen, you are going to assist me while rewarding yourselves. It is a win, win situation. You get to go back to England with your bounty and all I have to do is continue lying low and after a while I will return as the savior of Scottish whisky and the Glass name will be restored to its former glory.

That is why I have been farming wheat and barley. This will allow me to restart production immediately while the large breweries scratch their heads wondering what the hell happened. The smaller brewers will keep production going while I get my equipment in order. I will return from America with a lot of money, of course, the bulk of it will be some of the proceeds from the sale of the stolen loot. Yes, that's correct. You are going to find buyers and I want eighty percent. I have decided to fill the tank with my very own brew, the 'Tear Jerker', that alone will make you tens of thousands, so I am not exactly greedy, but I need the money to finance my plans. As I said, I will return from America to the rescue, I will buy out the smaller distilleries and build up from there. It will take my enemies years to catch up and Glass Whisky will be the flag bearer of Scottish Whisky.'

'That is a serious plan you have Mr. Glass and I am more than happy to be part of it. With that said, I am a willing participant in your great whisky heist,' said Randy followed by his annoying laughter.

'When do we begin?' asked Tony British. I have to make it back to London for a cockfight Sunday night. It is the biggest fight of the season and I don't want to miss it.'

'Don't be ridiculous,' scolded Glass. 'You are poised to earn the largest sum of cash in your miserable pitiful criminal career and you are over there thinking about a silly cockfight. Have you not heard a word I said? You are playing with the big boys now, no more chicken feed. Follow my instructions and you will be eating healthy for the rest of your miserable life and the same goes for all of you. And don't you dare think you can do a runner on me for my tentacles have no boundaries or loyalty. I can reach you anywhere you can imagine to hide and you will not get a chance to spend a pound. You will always be thinking is this the moment when John Glass will unleash his wrath. I can guarantee my friends; you will not see it coming. Believe me, many men have had that misguided thought and they are not around to talk about hindsight. Am I making myself clear?'

'Yes Sir,' responded the men in unison.

He continued, 'The heist will be the easy part, but keeping it a secret is the hard part. I trust that you have vetted each man around this table Victor? Glass looked at Vic, but Vic did not answer.

'That was a question Victor. Allow me to repeat, 'Do you trust all the men sitting around this table? Think carefully before you answer because it could be a matter of life or death. I cannot tolerate any parrots. I know that these men are greedy and where greed sleeps loyalty does not reside.'

Vic responded, 'I trust Randy, Fred and Harry are his close associates, so I trust them.'

Deep down he did not trust them, but he knew that if he said he didn't they may not see the light of day again. He continued, 'Tony British over there is not a snitch, Jamaicans have their special ways of dealing with informers and I am sure he will hold his tongue. Well you know McDougal, and by the sound of things I think you know him better than me. I thought I knew him, but you seem to know him very well, so he is your call.'

McDougal   started   to   look   uncomfortable   upon

hearing Vic's words. He could not believe that Vic did not vouch for him and he held his head down to hide his disappointment.

Vic noticed that he had placed McDougal in an awkward situation, so he said, 'Sorry McDougal, I had no idea that you knew John and by the sound of it, you two have a history together. You have never snitched on me, I know you as a principled man, but from what Glass said about you I must admit, I am a little disappointed that you snitched on him and his mate. But, it is in the past and I am sure you have learned from the mistakes you made as a young man. But again I must say, it is your call John,'

Glass looked at him and he knew that he had given the right answer. He dared not have vouched for McDougal and he knew that Glass was prepared to do something rash if he had out rightly said McDougal could be trusted a hundred percent.

John Glass spoke and said, 'Good answer Victor for if you had vouched for him I would have killed you both and Randy over there would take your place. I will trust McDougal this once, I don't really need him, but he is here so I guess he will be of some use and of course he managed to put the transport together, so he has a vested interest in the operation. If it goes belly up, the cops will surely trace the vehicles to him, so it is in his best interest to keep his glob shut.'

McDougal upon hearing Glass's approval was relieved that Glass would not hurt him and he held up his head, but he was still mindful of the fact that Glass was out for blood and it would be only a matter of time before he turned his attention to him. Now he had some time, he would play his part in the heist and get the money, and his liquor, of course, and disappear. He recalled he had agreed with Vic to only take some of the brew as payment and also that he was doing it for Francis, but now the game had changed. He had not expected to see Glass and now he was thinking about his survival. He would sell the garage and flee to Australia to live out the rest of his days in the outback, but what sense did that make? For Glass had declared that his tentacles were far reaching. He decided to play along for now, but he knew that eventually he would have to get rid of Glass in order to live a paranoia free life.

He looked Glass squarely in the eyes and said, 'Thank you for trusting me with this. I know that what I did in the past was an unforgivable act and I appreciate that you have greeted me with no hostility or prejudice. I will do my best to assist you in avenging your ancestors and I hope that it will be enough for you to forgive me. I want a guarantee that you will allow me to live in peace. I know you must have had your eyes on me all these years and I am also sure that you are aware that I lead a humble existence. I only came along on this expedition to help a friend in need and I have a close affinity to his dog Francis who saved my life on many occasions, so I owe it to him to get him back safe and unharmed.'

Glass responded, 'Yes, I know about the dog, but something tells me you would still be here with or without the disappearance of the animal. You missed your home country. You longed to taste the pure air of the highlands and bless your eyes on the beautiful hills and valleys. Welcome home old friend!'

McDougal looked at Glass and knew that he had anticipated his return and he seemed genuinely happy to see him. But, he would not be tricked into a false sense of security and he must always expect an attack. Glass himself knew that McDougal was dangerous that is why he was quick to relieve him of his pistol. He was in a permanent state of paranoia and he viewed everyone as hostile towards him and he could not afford to be struck down before he sabotaged the enemies of his ancestors. That is why he remained underground. He had to live long enough to figure out a way to carry on the bloodline. He hoped that he still had some healthy sperms swimming around inside his balls sack. Maybe there would come a time when they could be harvested and implanted in the right carrier whom he would handsomely reward to carry his seed. He even had some sinister thought about this, maybe the carrier would die in childbirth and by that happening all maternal ties would be severed and the children would be brought up by specially selected individuals. He restrained his thoughts as he remembered he was not alone and he did not want to divulge any details of his master plan. All the blokes in the room needed to know were the background to the heist and nothing else and they seemed content with the little he had already shared with them.

He said out loud, 'Alright then bring your attention back to the screen.' He pushed another command into what must be a universal remote control for it seemed to have controlled every gadget and electrical equipment in the place. The men were amazed to see a live feed on the screen and they were now looking at themselves.

Glass said, 'You see gentlemen I have this place all wired up, as a matter of fact I have the entire whisky country wired up or in this case wireless. I know a bloke at the space agency and with a few thousand quid I was able to set up my own home surveillance system. It is totally untraceable, unless you work for the space agency and even then it is still hard to detect because my feed is bouncing off the government's satellite, but the difference is that my chip gathers the video feed on Glasgow which gives me a clear view of whisky country. In the near future I am sure you will be able to log on to your computer and look at your house or your friend's house on the other side of the planet. For now this technology is only available to the military and those with the resources to pay for it. This should clearly indicate to you that I can find you anywhere on the planet hence my warning about developing any misguided ideas about absconding with the loot. Not many people can say they have.'

But how exactly does it work?' inquired Tony British

'It is easy; there are hundreds of satellites circling the planet. Most just take images of sites of interest that the government suspects of being a nuclear weapon plant, however, the images would come back distorted due to unpredictable weather conditions. Some hostile countries smarten up and started using mobile labs to do their research and it made it very difficult for our boys to keep track of them. So some smart bloke developed some powerful lens and satellites to bounce back live feeds, so we were able to track these mobile labs in real time and the SAS would go in and take them out one by one. Over time more powerful lenses were created and we were able to zoom in closer than before. We now have the technology to zoom in on a frog in the amazon. With this technology at my disposal I can tell you how many times my enemies visit the toilets every year. I can tell how many lorries of brew leave each distillery in whisky country on a daily basis. I know how much they are producing and I even know where the prized aged whisky barrels and crates are stored. Therefore, you will be able to go directly for the good stuff because you will have prior knowledge of where they are. This should take a couple hours off each raid. I can even remotely disconnect the cameras and replace the pictures with a static feed. The place will be yours for the night all you have to do is subdue the security guards and Bob's your uncle.'

The men now realized that Glass had planned the heist carefully. He imprisoned himself in his own home to scheme and to hide his presence from his neighbors. It was not easy getting Vic and his cohorts to his doorsteps and it was certainly not cheap. Each player had to be bought and who wasn't trusted met the same fate as the late Detective Alex Dawson.

He had instructed his operatives to subdue James Johnston, but he made it clear to them that he must be kept alive. Glass could not have allowed JJ to join Vic on the journey to Scotland for he knew that JJ would have seen the play the moment they entered whisky country. He had been there before many years ago and he knew where Glass lived. He would have alerted Vic to the fact that it was a set up and the plan would have suffered a major setback and he would have had to go back to the drawing board.

'Each of you will be given a listening device. You will not be able to communicate with me as I will be doing all the talking. If you follow my instructions then this should be a quick and efficient operation,' said Glass handing each man a hearing piece.

He waited for the men to inspect the devices they held in their hands and then he said, 'Listen to me carefully; none of the security guards should be seriously harmed or injured. The police view robbery as a minor offence, but accompanied by assault is a very serious crime and they will not stop until they expend every resource at their disposal to find the perpetrators. They will give up on the robbery offence in a few weeks when they cannot find any leads, so don't give them a reason to pursue you. Make sure your hands never leave your gloves, don't even take a piss or spit anywhere on the grounds or the interior of the distilleries. You will each wear overalls that will not leave any traces of fabric for the forensic blokes. These must be destroyed once you are safely out of the parameters of whisky country. You see gentlemen; I want it to look like an inside job. The police will be busy interviewing the employees and former disgruntled employees for the last decade and woe unto the man who doesn't have a perfect alibi.'

'What about the owners, will they not be after us as well?' asked Vic.

'That's a very good question Victor,' responded Glass. 'The answer is yes, they will still be looking for you even after the police have given up. They will hire private detectives, hit men and informers. They will search every nook and cranny of Great Britain. They will have eyes and ears in every pub and off license in the land.'

Glass thought for a moment and then he looked at Vic and Vic looked back in anticipation of a question.

Glass said, 'Vic, have you explored the basement of your pub?'

'Yes I have,' replied Vic. 'The person who built it was a bloke named Patrick Carlisle and he seemed to have used the place to store his old furniture and antiques. I think the place is large enough to stash the loot.'

'Good,' said Glass. 'I want you to store the loot inside as soon as you get back to London. Then I want you all to lay low for a month. Just continue living your decrepit lives and by doing so, I am sure no one will suspect you miserable lot of pulling of the greatest whisky heist in modern history. Vic it is your responsibility to get the whisky stretched and bottled and I am sure you know someone who can assist with that. After which I want you to find trusted wholesalers to sell the brew or better yet it would be ideal to only deal with one buyer, an exporter preferably. The sooner we get it off the island the better. These brewers know their stuff and with one whiff they will be able to tell that it is theirs.'

He noticed a look of confusion on their faces especially the greedy Harry and Fred.

'Ok, allow me to retort,' said Glass. 'Hide the whisky as soon as you get back to London, get it stretched and rebottled, find an exporter and get rid of the brew, put the money in a safe place and wait for me to make contact. I hope my instructions are clear for we will not speak in person again until after the heist and please do remember I am always watching.'

'I have a question,' said McDougal with his hands waving in the air.

'What is it?' snapped Glass. 'You better not ask an operational question for I have already told you what you need to know and the rest of the instructions will be conveyed through the listening devices. What could you possibly need to know old chap?'

McDougal hesitated as if he no longer wanted to ask the question, but he was compelled to do so.

'What I want to know is why don't you hide the whisky here? It is closer and it would mean that we could make multiple trips. And instead of contaminating the aged barrels you could hide them for the next twenty years and your cavern is the perfect place. You could then use Port Glasgow, which is a small low key port to get the whisky out of the region. If we do it your way then there is a high risk of us losing the whole lot whether it is to the cops, the Italians, the Jamaicans or any other opportunist who just happen to find out about it? Why take the risk?' McDougal asked bravely.

'I represent the Jamaicans and I am here,' interjected Tony British giving McDougal a cross look.

'Ah McDougal,' sighed Glass. 'Let me ask you this. Why would I want to steal from my backyard and then hide the contraband out front?'

It was a rhetorical question, but McDougal responded none the less. He said, 'Because no one would suspect it and with your level of secrecy I can assume that no one really knows about this place.'

'But you are wrong Sam!' said Glass. 'You all now know about this place and I have told you most of my plans. What will prevent any of you in this room from ratting me out? I am not comfortable with that, so I think it is best if you keep the loot and you take responsibility if you get caught. What will prevent us from implicating you if we are caught you may ask? The answer is, my no good son of a rake ex son-in-law tried to rob me and I have the video to prove it detective. When he found that Glass whisky was out of operation to his disappointment and embarrassment he could not leave Scotland empty handed after the long journey he had subjected his men to, so he decided to rob some of the distilleries in the region. He also made it look like sabotage, doing this to further implicate me.'

The men were astonished to hear Glass making up the story that he would tell the police if he was implicated. He turned to Vic and said, 'You see Victor, the family feuds are narrowly known and anyone who still has knowledge of the history may just point their finger in the right direction, even if the argument sounds like conspiracy theory someone may develop an interest and follow the scent. This may lead to a search of my premises and they may discover this secret abode and that must not happen.'

Vic gave Glass a nod of understanding and Glass nodded back. He now turned his attention back to McDougal and said, 'So, the answer to your question Mr. McDougal is, no. I will not store the whisky on my premises and we are certainly not shipping it from Port Glasgow. I want to put as many miles between me and the loot as possible. There must not be any traces, I cannot stress that enough.'

'I understand,' said a verbally defeated McDougal.

'Have you ever heard about six degrees of separation?' asked Glass. 'Well, I am the epitome of that. That's the art of doing successful business and as the Italians would put it; you have to know a guy who knows a guy who knows something about it and that means anything or anybody. You don't get successful by doing things all by yourself you have to know people with the skills and expertise you desire for your trade, whether it is legal or criminal. Knowing people is the first step and it's easy, but the difficulty lies with getting them to do what you want and for that you need to have a little knowledge of psychology and be verse in the art of cunning. Victor over there is a natural as I am and this is why he is sitting in this room tonight. I am giving him one chance to show me that he is worthy to sit among the masters of shrewd. But, enough of this, it is now 9:00 pm get ready to move out at ten.'

The men were now actually growing fond of John Glass. The few hours spent with him thought them a lot of what can be achieved in this world. The wealth that they saw was unimaginable to them before tonight and they finally admitted to themselves that they were merely small timers. They could not comprehend the full extent or impact of Glass's plans, but they didn't need to know for this would be the biggest job of their criminal careers and if they pleased him then they would be sure to be called up for future jobs.

'Now that everybody is clear, let us get on with it', announced Glass. He led the men out of the room in the direction of the elevator. They were now eager and motivated to proceed with the operation.

'Do you have any food up there?' inquired Tony

British. 'I am starving. Even a slice of toast and a cuppa would do the trick, besides we will be doing some heavy lifting and that cannot be done on an empty stomach,' he lamented.

'Yes, there is food up in the house, I got something especially for you and I guarantee you will have enough energy to lift an elephant,' said Glass.

'Sounds good to me,' said Tony British.

The men exited the elevator and were now facing a spiraling staircase going upwards. They mounted the stairs and found themselves back in the farm house.

'The kitchen is over there, go help yourselves. There is chicken, turkey, mash potatoes, roast beef and vegetables,' said Glass.

The men proceeded to the kitchen without hesitation and they each grabbed a large plate and utensils. They tucked in like ravenous beasts for they were all hungry. They devoured the meal without hesitation and the second serving disappeared from the plate at the same speed as the first. Glass joined them at the table, but he merely picked his food for he had other things on his mind.

As if a bulb has been lit in Vic's mind and with its illumination brought forth a question to his lips. 'Tell me John,' he said. 'You said you have been locked in for months, so who takes care of the dogs and the maintenance of the property?' he asked.

To Vic's surprise, Glass's answer was not hostile; instead he smiled and said, 'I have a guy who takes care of things for me. He comes in once a week and check up on things up here and to bring me food and supplies. He is a good lad and I trust him. His family and I have been very close and he is like the son I wish I had.'

'So where is he now?' inquired Randy.

'Don't worry about that. Just remember that the eye is

always watching,' responded Glass.

The men then scanned the room for cameras and noticed that they were there monitoring their every move. They also now developed the notion that they were being watched by hidden eyes. There was another player in the game and they had no idea who it was, but whoever it was would have seen their faces and this gave Glass an extra layer of protection. Perhaps it was a hit man that was prepared to take them out one by one after the job was complete. The men held the thoughts in their heads as they devoured the third serving of food.

'Ok lads, fifteen minutes to show time,' announced Glass. 'The tanker is already loaded with my famous 'Tear Jerker'. It is the special stuff, so it must be protected at all cost for it alone is worth tens of thousands of pounds and I am entrusting its safe arrival in London to you Victor.'

Vic nodded in acknowledgement and acceptance of the responsibility.

Glass said, 'You will be robbing three distilleries tonight and I have logged in their coordinates in this GPS device, so that you can locate them easily. You have six hours to do the job, that is two hours at each distillery and I will notify you when the two hours is up. I want you all on the M74 by 4am and you should be on the M6 before daybreak making your way to the M1. Including rest time, you should be back in London in time for Sunday tea.'

The men got up from the table and was about to exit the farmhouse when Tony British inquired about the dogs and their whereabouts. The men paused in their tracks upon the mention of dogs and they allowed Glass to proceed before them. He assured them that the animals had been subdued and the coast was clear. He told them that they would only attack on his command. The men proceed to where the lorries were parked and

Glass informed them that the gas tanks were filled up and extra fuel was loaded, so that they would not have to stop at filling stations to refuel. This made the men even more convinced that there was another player assisting Glass with the coordination of the heist, but the person remained hidden and they may never know his identity.

Vic observed the device in his hand with the letters GPS etched above the glass screen. On the screen he noticed a cluster of three tiny green arrows trained at a particular point on a map. Below he noticed a single flashing red arrow pointing in the direction of the three flashing green arrows. He had never seen or heard about this device and wondered how it worked. 'John, what does the letters GPS stands for?' he turned to Glass and asked. 'I have never seen anything like this before. What exactly does it do?'

'The letters stands for Global Positioning System,' replied Glass. 'It is used by the military to keep track of its submarines and ships where ever they are in the world. It also is an instrumental tool used in wars to ensure that missiles hit their intended targets to minimize collateral damage. I am sure in a few years every vehicle in Britain will have one of these devices, but for now only a very few privileged individuals can get their hands on this technology.'

'Interesting!' exclaimed Vic. 'And you think that they will eventually put this in the hand of ordinary people?'

'Yes, they will.' replied Glass. 'Whoever first roles this out to the general population will become a billionaire as everybody will want one. All the frustration arising from the plotting of routes on large paper maps will be totally eradicated. The driver will only need to punch in his destination and the GPS will direct him there. I have already punched in the coordinates to the three distilleries, so all you have to do is follow the arrows.'

'Ok,' responded Vic. 'How will we subdue the security guards? From what I have seen from your CCTV footage of the distilleries each has at least two security guards.'

Glass answered and said, 'You are going to drive the fuel truck up to the gates and tell the guards you are there to deliver fuel. They will of course be suspicious of the fact that you turned up in the middle of the night, but you will tell them that you got a flat and you had to stop and change it. You can even agree to make them check in with the Shell depot and rest assured everything will check out. We will intercept the call and confirm the delivery. When the gates are open your men will rush in, grab the guards and tie them up.'

'What about dogs? Surely there must be some,' asked Tony British.

'Yes there are many dogs on the premises, but they are caged,' responded Glass. 'They keep them locked up, but they can be released with the push of a button. That is why you have to rush in and grab the guards quickly before they get a chance to push the button to free the dogs. I will be monitoring the premises, so I will tell you the positions of the guards. This will enable you to carry out the operation swiftly and without obstructions. Go on then gentlemen, mount up and good luck.'

The men proceeded towards their vehicles as soon as Glass gave the order. Vic noticed that the dogs were not around and he also noticed that the body of the late Detective Dawson was no longer lying in the position where it had fallen. Now he was certain Glass had company and this notion increased when his peripheral vision picked up a silhouette moving quickly away from the upstairs farmhouse window. He did not react to what he has seen because he knew that Glass had his eyes on him. He opened the door of the tanker and entered. He took the opportunity to look at the farmhouse one last time, but he did not see any movements or signs of life coming from the building. It just stood there in the darkness just as he had approached it, it looked empty and desolate.

'I will be communicating with you all the time, I will be your eyes all you have to do is follow my instructions.' shouted Glass.

Vic waved at him and started his maneuver to get the oil tanker facing the exit of the premises. He checked the GPS device and the red arrow pointed in the direction he should go. The other men started their lorries and followed behind slowly. The six men were finally on their way to carry out the greatest whisky heist since prohibition. A figure emerged from the darkness and stood beside Glass as the lights of the lorries grew dim in the distance.

'Do you trust them?' asked the mysterious companion. 'After all, they are nothing but a bunch of plebs.'

'Vic is smart, so I am sure he would not try to double cross us just yet, not until after the merchandise is in his hands. After that I am afraid that's when he will become unpredictable and as for his associates I don't trust any of them. They might double cross him before he gets a chance to double cross us,' said the second companion.

Glass looked at them and laughed out loudly.

He said, 'Everything is working according to plan, they are still puzzled by the things I have told them and from what they have seen. We just need to maintain control over the operation and everything will be ok. Now get back to London and ensure that everything is in order and remember we need eyes in the basement of the pub for that is the only blind spot and that is where they will store the whisky. I want to see and know everything.'

The second companion obeyed and left immediately.

Glass and the other companion went back to the farmhouse and headed straight to the room with the surveillance equipment.

✄ 23 ✄

SHOW TIME

It *was little after 10:00 pm when* the men re-entered the densely populated area of whisky country. The place was still dark and quiet just as it had been when they first drove through. Vic wondered what would really drive a man to the extremes that Glass had gone through to exact a revenge of this nature. He could agree with stealing the whisky after all that is why he was there, but the bit he could not understand was contaminating the barrels. That's just cruel and even blasphemous in the eyes of men such as Sam McDougal and James Johnston who loved their whisky. The bloke must either be extremely wise or a total mad man who was obsessed with revenge.

Vic still had a lot of unanswered questions, but they would have to wait for he had work to do. His thoughts were disturbed by a crackling sound in his right ear. It was Glass shuffling around making himself ready to oversee the operation of his long planned whisky heist.

Glass said, 'Come in Victor, I am tracking the lorries. Look at the GPS; you are two miles away from the first mark. I want you to drive up to the gate with confidence and blow the horn. You will have to get out and speak to the security guard through the intercom; he will be checking the monitors and will not come to the gate until he thinks it is safe. There are two guards protecting this distillery and they are both armed, so you have to be cautious. Make sure the other lorries are out of sight, the cameras have a three hundred and sixty degrees view of the perimeter of the property. Stop a little way before and let the men hide in the cabin of the tanker, and they must be prepared to pounce in an instant. Tell the guards what I had told you to say earlier. They will indeed follow security protocol and call it in and they will discover that a delivery of petrol was scheduled, but the only suspicion will be that it is late. They will check with the Guvnor and he will give clearance. I have tapped into the telephone system and any calls they make will come to me.'

Vic signaled the other lorries to pull over a mile before they reached the distillery. They reviewed Glass's instructions and agreed that it was not a bad plan. Vic figured that since it was the first distillery they only needed one lorry, so he decided to let McDougal stay behind and wait for the signal to proceed.

McDougal protested, and boasting of his tiger-like agility in situations such has these. The men all laughed at McDougal's impersonation of Mohammad Ali's 'float like a butterfly, sting like a bee' dance. McDougal quietly acknowledged his futile attempt to look tough. He may have been a dangerous bloke in his youth, but old age had defeated him and he agreed to listen out for the signal. The other four robbers hid themselves in the cabin of the oil tanker. It was a tight fit, and Tony British protested about the limited space and his discomfort with 'rubbing up' against so many blokes. Vic told him to shut up and be ready to take down the security guards.

The tanker approached the distillery owned by the descendants of the Paisley estate. They were Glass's first target, and Vic wondered what their sins were. It wasn't the largest distillery they had seen during their way through whisky country, but it was a decent size, much larger than a lot of the others. As he maneuvered the vehicle up the rise to the main gate he saw the large gold crested coat of arms he had seen earlier on Glass's monitor. It was sitting atop a large arch which sat on the back of two large well sculptured lions on either side of the entrance. He also noticed two large cameras focused directly on the vehicle and this made him a bit uneasy.

Once again Vic heard the crackling sound in his ear, but he had quickly learned that it was Glass's way of notifying him of his arrival at the proverbial dictatorial podium. He said, 'Vic, listen carefully. The contaminant is under the passenger seat. Handle it with care because it is extremely toxic. You only need to put one drop in each barrel and the whisky will be contaminated in seconds. I want you to personally handle it. For tonight my dear Victor, you shall be my right hand.'

This made Vic uncomfortable and he just realized the enormity of the consequences if the contaminated whisky were bottled and distributed before the apparent sabotage was discovered. He was now upset not only with the fact that he will be an accomplice to a possible mass murder, but his heist was being hijacked by his father in law who he hadn't seen in years, the same guy who didn't even turn up to his daughter's funeral. '*What manner of beast is this man*?' He thought.

He opened the door and exited the lorry. His nostrils were immediately filled with the scent of barley. He went up to the intercom and spoke to the security guard who dutifully went through the security checks and got clearance to let the oil tanker in. The guard pressed the button and the huge gate opened. The second guard with his Remington rifle in hand proceeded towards Vic and instructed him to hold his hands to the air. He frisked Vic and then instructed him to get back in the lorry while he carried out a bomb check. The guard then reached in his pocket and took out a small device. Vic sat in the vehicle and he watched the guard through the rear view mirrors. The guard pointed his device underneath the lorry and Vic could see a red laser beam flickering. The guard carried out the security check for about five minutes and then he approached the driver's seat of the lorry and instructed Vic to proceed. As Vic maneuvered the lorry onto the grounds of the distillery his heart started to race and he thought to himself, this is it, no turning back. He checked his mirrors and noticed that both guards were approaching and he instructed the men to get ready. As the guards approached the doors of the lorry Vic popped it open and started talking, giving them no chance to get a word in.

He said, 'This has got to be the worst night of my life. I had not one, but two flats. Imagine me all by myself trying to change these monstrosities. I gave up the task after about an hour and I had to wait another hour for the blokes from the AA to turn up. It took four of them one hour to change the bloody things! Sorry I am late lads.'

Before either of the guards could say a word the men pounced on them. Randy commandeered the Remington and Tony British relieved the other guard of his Browning. Both sustained minor injuries, but nothing to call the funeral directors about. The robbers gagged the guards and led them to the entrance of the main distillery building. Vic instructed them to open the door and they obeyed. Their eyes were filled with fright and terror and all they could do was mumble some unrecognized dialect. Randy gave them a smack on the head and told them to shut it.

Vic radioed McDougal and instructed him to bring in the lorry. As the men entered the distillery they were mesmerized by the sheer volume of whisky they saw. There were hundreds of bottles labeled up and ready to be boxed and shipped.

'We have to move fast,' said Vic. 'We have less than two hours to get the lorry loaded, so no time wasting or gimmicks from you lot.'

He left the men to get on with it and went back to get the contaminant from the tanker. McDougal arrived while Vic was ascending from the steps of the cabin and he could see the excitement in his eyes.

McDougal said, 'How were things with the guards? Was it easy?'

'It was very easy,' replied Vic.

'Old Glass sure knows how to cook a pot,' said McDougal

'He sure does,' said Vic. 'I don't trust the bastard though. Go to the security station and keep an eye on the monitors.'

'Can I at least take a look inside?' asked McDougal. 'I haven't been inside a distillery in decades.'

Vic replied, 'Ok, but only for a minute. We have to get this done quickly and we don't want any surprises. We don't want the master blender to turn up because he forgot his nose, so just one look and then take up your post in the guard's station and don't even think about asking for a drink.'

The men entered the distillery and found the other robbers waiting. McDougal was satisfied with what he saw and he soaked up the atmosphere. He then left, but not before hiding a small bottle of whisky in his jacket. Vic saw what he did, but decided to allow the old man to indulge and reminisce on his young days in Scotland. Furthermore, Vic knew that the size bottle McDougal lifted would not have any impact on his vision; it would only quench his thirst for a little while.

Vic said, 'Ok lads! Let us get on with it; the lorry should be able to hold everything that is already bottled up. Randy and Tony British go get those two forklifts parked over there. Harry and Fred start putting the bottles in those boxes and then pack them on the pallets.'

He then left them and went in search of the oak barrels. He found them sitting peacefully with its contents awaiting their turn to grace the lips of a whisky lover somewhere in the world. He searched for the light switch and he flipped it. As the illumination covered the room he was amazed at the amount of barrels he saw and it would take him the entire time to contaminate all of them. He decided that he would instruct the men to load a few of them.

He approached the first barrel and removed the bung from the bung hole. He uncorked the cover of the three litre bottle of green liquid he held in his hand and discovered that the cover was equipped with a drip tube. He remembered that Glass had told him that one drop would do. He removed the cork full from the bottle and he held the drip tube above the bung hole, so he could control the drops. A single drop escaped from the mouth of the drip tube and fell into the barrel. Vic could hear the bubbling reaction as the mysterious green liquid made contact with the whisky. He didn't waste a minute and one after the other he contaminated all the barrels except for the ones he decided to steal. Years of fermentation was disturbed and corrupted in less than a second and he knew that it would take this distillery a long time to recover. When he was finished the bottle barely felt lighter, however, thousands of gallons of pure Scottish whisky had been rendered putrid and not safe for consumption. Vic rejoined the other men and noticed that they were almost finished. He instructed Randy and Tony British to get the barrels loaded and he helped Harry and

Fred with loading the pallets. In no time the raid on the first distillery had been completed without complications, but for the guards who have been gagged, tied up and placed in a dark room and would not be found until Monday morning when the brewers got in.

Vic heard the now familiar crackling sound of Glass making his presence known.

He said, 'Well done Victor! I am impressed. I have already replaced the CCTV footage erasing any evidence that you were there. The brewers and coppers will be scratching their heads for days as they will not see anything suspicious on the tapes. They will naturally blame the guards, but all this is dependent on how clean you do the next two jobs. The next mark is a mile up the road. It is the Dumbarton place and they also have two guards, so use the same strategy to subdue them. The Dumbarton place produces the same volume of whisky as the Paisley place, so again you will only need one lorry for the job.'

Again Vic and his accomplices executed the plan with precision and they now had two lorries filled with Scottish whisky most of which were special blends. Randy said, 'Not a bad days work I can almost feel the money in my hands. What are you going to do with your share Vic?'

Vic looked at him and said, 'Are you really thinking about that when we are still in the woods?'

Randy laughed and said, 'Why don't we just forget about the third brewery and do a runner?'

Vic replied and said, 'Do that and we will be hunted like animals. I am surprised to hear that from you Randy, I thought that stupid notion would come from Harry, Fred or even Tony British over there, but not you. We are going to finish the job and then we will decide our move when we get back to London. Besides we have three more lorries to fill and I suspect that the last distillery is the mother ship. Glass is smart and precise, so we will follow his orders and see what we can salvage for ourselves. He knew that there is the possibility of us doing a runner as you suggested, so I suspect that he gave us some of his own special whisky to tie us in. Even if we keep the whisky we lift from the distilleries, we will still owe him for his and he will do everything in his power to ensure that we don't cross him. You saw how he operates; he is one sinister son of a gun.'

Randy said, 'Ok Vic, we will follow his orders through, but I am not doing this for free I can assure you of that.'

Vic said, 'Well, I am not doing it for free either. I am doing it for Francis and I know you know how much that dog means to me. I was totally shattered when I read the note about his kidnap and I almost died when I found the bloody ear. I am doing it for him; I am doing it for my best friend. I have been calm and patient about it all along, but if they kill him, I am going to unleash a reign of terror on anybody who even as much as heard about the kidnapping.'

McDougal overheard the conversation and joined in. He said, 'You can count me in for I too love that dog and I am doing this for him also.'

Vic now had a forlorn look on his face as he thought about Francis and the time they had together. The animal literally saved his life many times when he was sinking deeper into his depression. After the spell at Bedlam, Francis helped him with his readjustment in society and in no time he was completely off medication. He didn't need Hyde after all for Francis thought him a valuable lesson about caring and having responsibility.

Vic heard Glass's signal and he waited for his next set of instructions. Glass said, 'Well done Victor! The Kilbride place is next and this will be the most difficult. I was not able to install my surveillance equipment inside the compound, so I am not too sure what their security system is like. I was only able to get a camera pointing at the main entrance of the property. I haven't seen anybody come out since this evening when the brewers left for the weekend. You are still making good time, so this should allow you to deal with any surprises or disruptions to the plan. One thing I am sure is that they have guard dogs and they are not as obedient as mine and they have an automated release system attached to the kennels that will open the gate once the censors are released. I have that system myself, so I do not doubt it that Kilbride has the same.'

'Oh no, not more dogs,' said Tony British. 'How are we going to deal with them Vic?' he asked.

Vic replied and said, 'I do not know, it all depends on how many there are and where they are stationed.'

'Let us put some of the contaminant in their watering system. I am sure it will easily take them down,' suggested Tony British.

'I don't think I could hurt a dog,' said Vic. 'I love dogs, after all that is why we are here tonight.'

Tony British said, 'You may not be able to do it, but I certainly can. I hate dogs and I think they are the vilest creatures on the face of the earth. I am talking from experience here mate, I swear to God every dog have it in for me. Ever since I was a young lad I could not bear to be in the presence of them, they give me the creeps and if I might add, I have been bitten quite a lot and I have the scars to prove it.'

The men all looked in disbelief when Tony British lifted his right trouser foot to reveal his leg; a large chunk of which was missing.

He said, 'See I tell you, I am talking from experience and by the size of that distillery it doesn't take a stretch of the imagination to figure out what breed of dogs they have protecting the premises.'

Randy laughed and said, 'This is your chance to exact your revenge on the relations of your nemesis.'

Tony British replied and said, 'That particular nemesis of mine is no longer around as I dealt with him immediately after he ripped out a piece of my leg. I don't know if it was reflex or adrenaline, but I choked the bastard to death.'

Vic said, 'That is just cruel mate and the sad bit is that the poor animal was only reacting to you trespassing. You thieving bastard'

Tony British said, 'If you live in a glass house don't throw stones and you are in Glass's house right now, so don't be quick to call me a thief for we are of the same fraternity. Admittedly, I am not the smartest criminal, but I get by and this scar on my leg is a testament of my hard work. Furthermore, I am no longer working for you Vic. I hope you haven't forgotten your friends the Mussolini brothers.'

Vic was now trapped in thought. He was so induced by Glass that he had forgotten his other enemies. He had forgotten that Tony British was not his best friend and the Mussolini brothers would surely kill him if he did not pay up is debt before the deadline. He was surrounded by sharks, they were nothing but bloody opportunist, and he knew that they would throw him under the bus without giving it a second thought if the right price and opportunity was presented to them. For now they are his allies, his comrades in crime and they still needed to finish the job. He asked himself many questions. Glass was smart; he targeted the biggest and the best breweries. Surely he must have had more enemies than Paisley, Dumbarton and Kilbride. Why them? What was so special about these three families that he would go to these extremes for revenge? He knew that the Kilbride job would be the most damaging as it was the largest distillery and as such they will suffer the most lost. Glass could not gain access to this distillery which indicated that security was tight and it also told Vic that the Kilbride's knew they had enemies.

Glass pulled Vic from his thoughts saying, 'Why are you stationary Victor? Proceed with the operation. This time I want you to bring all six vehicles up to the distillery and I want you to load the three empty lorries and fill every available space in the others. When you are finished I don't want you to contaminate the barrels, but instead I want you to burn the place to the ground. Use some of the Tear Jerker to start the fire, and they will think one of the copper pots exploded as a result of too much pressure caused by negligence on the part of the brewer charged with setting up the automated distillation reactors. However, do not use a lot of my brew because it is by far the most valuable and besides once the fire reaches the distillation room, the entire place will go up in flames and you might want to be as far away as possible when that happens. The Kilbride place is located on the edge of the M74, so you will be on your way back to London in a matter of minutes. I have disengaged their electronics, so the dogs will be immobilized, but that will not prevent them from making a lot of noise. Also, I have another piece of technology to introduce you to, it is called a Taser Gun and I have placed them in the glove compartment of the oil tanker. Go and get them and I will give you the instructions.'

Vic retrieved the black objects from the glove compartment of the tanker and went over to where the other robbers were standing and said, 'Glass wants us to use these on this job.'

'What are they?' inquired Randy.

'He said they are called Taser Guns,' replied Vic.

'I have never heard of such weapons,' said Randy

'He is going to give us the instructions,' said Vic

Glass started to speak again and said, 'The Taser gun is still in the development stages, so not many people are aware of the existence of such a device. It delivers an electrical charge so powerful it could take down an elephant, and it all depends on the voltage the shooter wishes to expend on his target. It can be set to fire up to 150, 000 volts of electricity and you don't want be on the receiving end of that. Go on try it out on Randy, he is a big bloke, I am sure he can handle it. Use the up down arrows on the side of the gun to set the voltage. You only have one chance to take down your target, so make it count. Otherwise, it will take you about five minutes to reset it so it can fire again.'

Vic pointed the Taser gun in the direction of Randy who immediately ran for cover, but he was not fast enough. Vic pressed the trigger releasing what looked like electric wires which seemed to have latched on to Randy's back. Randy fell to the ground shaking like he was having a seizure. Vic released the trigger and Randy's ordeal abruptly ended.

'How did it work?' inquired Glass.

'It worked perfectly well,' replied Vic

'I thought we couldn't communicate with him,' said McDougal.

Vic placed a finger on his lips and then smiled as he realized that for the first time Glass had made a mistake. He could hear them all along. He fooled them into believing that there was only a one way communication, so that he could listen for dissention. But he dropped his guard by asking a direct question. Fred went over to Randy and removed the wires from his back. He then tried to help him to his feet, but Randy was not happy. He grabbed Fred and threw him several meters from where they were standing.

Vic said laughing, 'Calm down Randy, at least we have weapons that won't cause any serious damage, only a brief moment of shock.'

'Ok, now recoil the wires and reset the device, and remember you will only have time for one shot, so make it count,' said Glass.

Randy was back to normal and he even gave out a small version of his hyena sounding laugh as a sign of no hard feelings. Vic handed the men the other five Taser Guns and confirmed that they understood how to use them. The men answered in the affirmative as they inspected their new weapons.

Vic said, 'We are going to drive right through the gates, all six of us. The moment you pass through the gate, I want you to start looking out for guards. Do not wait for them to come to you, instead, alight from your vehicle as you enter the compound and choose your target. Let us pray that there are not more than six guards otherwise someone will be seriously hurt. If you miss just use your fists. Ok lads, mount up and let us do this. Oh, and don't worry about the dogs, Glass has disabled the security system, so they won't be able to leave their kennel.'

The men all rushed to their vehicles and were now on their way to do the hit on the Kilbride place. The Kilbride whisky distillery was the largest they have seen in whisky country, and the sheer magnitude of the place was breathtaking. No way the three empty lorries would be able to carry the entire stock that laid waiting inside, hence Glass's plan to destroy the building itself and make it look like an accident.

Tony British drove the lorry with the hardest front end, so he took the lead. Upon approaching the entrance of the distillery he accelerated and the vehicle rammed into the gate with such a force that it tore away the columns holding it up. McDougal who was trailing behind narrowly missed being hammered by a huge concrete slab which went flying in the direction of his lorry. All the lorries made it through the gate unscathed and the men immediately alighted, but to their surprise, they did not see a living soul.

Randy said, 'This smells like a set up. A distillery of this magnitude should have security guards? Let us get the hell out of here.'

Vic said, 'Wait a minute. Did you hear that?'

'The only thing I can hear is a metal door slamming in my face. I really don't like the feel of this,' said Randy.

Vic said, 'Shut up and listen.'

McDougal said, 'Yes, I can hear something. I recognize the accent, it sounds like whisky talk.'

'Are there people inside?' asked Tony British. 'There goes the element of surprise; I nearly took off McDougal's head back there.'

Vic said, 'I don't think they heard us; otherwise they would have been out here already.'

Vic went up to the window where the talking was coming from. He looked inside and saw some men playing cards and drinking whisky. He smiled and went back to where the other robbers were standing.

He said, 'Listen up, there are seven of them inside, they are playing cards and drinking whisky. Take out your Taser guns and set it to 50, 000 volts, get ready and wait for me to fire first.'

Vic kicked the door in and rushed in the direction where the men were sitting. 'Stay where you are or I will shoot you down!' he shouted.

The surprised men froze in their seats and awaited their next set of instructions from the men with strange looking weapons in their hands. The other robbers took up their positions and all the men were covered except the one in the three piece suit. There were three men dressed in security guard uniforms and the other three looked like they were regular brewers. The man in the three piece suit looked distinguished which he confirmed when he spoke.

He said, 'What on earth is going on here? How dare you trespass on my property! Who are you?'

'That is irrelevant,' replied Vic. 'We are here for the whisky.'

The man eyes were steaming with anger and he looked Vic in the eyes and said, 'What is that in your hand? Is it some sort of toy?'

'No it is not a toy,' replied Vic

Vic looked around the table and set his eyes upon the biggest security guard who looked like he could match Randy pound for pound. He then pressed the trigger of the Taser Gun and the electrodes went flying in the direction of the huge security guard. The electrodes connected with his stomach and he went into an immediate seizure and keeled over backwards. The other men looked at their colleague and then immediately looked back at the weapon in Vic's hand. Vic released the trigger and the security guard was knocked out cold.

Vic said, 'You see my old friend, it is not a toy. He then went over to the security guard and removed the electrodes from his chest. He then reset the weapon and pointed it at the man in the three piece suit.

The man in the three piece suit looked Vic squarely in the eyes for the first time. He knitted his brow and kept his eyes focused on Vic.

He said, 'you look familiar, do I know you?'

Vic replied, 'I don't think so, I have never seen you before.'

'Oh yes, now I remember,' the man said nodding his head. 'I was at your wedding. You married John Glasgow's daughter. I heard about the accident, such a tragedy.'

Vic looked closer at the man, but he still did not recognize him. The man broke the silence and said, 'Where is that son of a bitch John Glass? I haven't seen him in more than a decade. What the hell is going on here? Did he send you to rob me?'

'I am right here and I have always been here,' announced Glass appearing suddenly and pointing a revolver at the man in the three piece suit. 'Kenny Kilbride, it has been a long time. It is a pleasure seeing you under such circumstances. I want back what your father stole from my mine. Where are the bottles?'

'They are not here,' responded Kenny Kilbride. 'They are locked up in my house in East Stirling.'

'No they are not,' said Glass. 'I have already looked. As a matter of fact I looked everywhere. I am happy that you admitted to having them otherwise I would have had to resort to torture. Look, I have been searching for the Scotsman for years and you had them all along. The worst part of it is that you pretended to be my friend, but you have been deceiving me all this time, but it ends here tonight.'

'What is the Scotsman?' asked a puzzled Vic.

'There is no time to tell you Victor, but maybe I will in the future,' replied Glass. 'What I can tell you is that his father double crossed mine. My father was a master blender, the best in Scotland, and he created a blend that has yet to be duplicated. Unfortunately he died tragically in a blast that occurred in his lab and the recipe and method of distillation died with him. We found out that the blast occurred as a result of sabotage and the only ever batch of his secret blend was stolen. I have been searching for it ever since I became aware of its existence.

The Scotsman became legendary due to its elusiveness, but I am sure Mr. Kilbride and his friends have had the privilege of sampling it'

Glass cocked the revolver and said, 'I am serious Kilbride. Where are the bottles? Are they here?'

'Do you think I would be stupid enough to hide the Scotsman here? You will never find the bottles and I am getting closer to replicating the blend. I am going to make millions and there is nothing you can do about it.'

A now furious Glass said, 'If I cannot have it then neither will you.'

He pulled the trigger and shot Kilbride in the chest. Kilbride looked at Vic and tried to say something, but his mouth was quickly filling with blood. He pushed a button, but nothing dramatic happened. Glass smiled and said, 'I have disengaged your electronic system, so your guard dogs won't be coming to your aid. You are going to die tonight if you don't tell me where you hid the Scotsman.'

Through the blood Kilbride spluttered, 'I will never tell you. You are an evil man.'

He looked at Vic with dazed eyes. His life energy was depleting quickly.

He said, 'Go on son ask him how exactly his daughter died.'

Before Vic could react to Kilbride's statement another shot echoed in his ears. This time the shot got Kilbride in his heart and he died immediately. Vic turned to look at Glass, but he was already looking at him.

Glass said, 'What? Are you really paying attention to what that old fool was saying? He wanted to save his skin and you know a cornered man will say anything to save his hide.'

Vic noticed that the revolver was now pointing in his direction and Glass had a sinister look in his eyes.

Vic said, 'What I was going to say is, what about the

other men? They have seen our faces.'

Glass replied, 'Tie them up; we are leaving them in here with the late Kenny Kilbride. The security guards and the brewers pleaded for mercy, but their pleas fell on deaf ears. Glass instructed the robbers to Taser them. Harry and Fred requested that they be handed the task of electrocuting the men. The permission was granted and they took pleasure in seeing the men flutter like dying birds on the floor. 'How many volts did you give them?' asked Randy.

'One hundred thousand,' replied Fred laughing hysterically.

'You crazy bastards,' said Randy.

Glass said, 'Come on, time is going, start loading up the lorries while I go look for my property.'

The men moved with haste as they loaded the three empty lorries with Kilbride's whisky. They were almost finished when they heard a loud joyous scream.

'Yes, I found it!' shouted Glass. 'Come here Victor and feast your eyes on these babies.'

Vic went over to where Glass was standing and took the bottle that Glass held in his hand.

'Be careful,' said Glass. 'One bottle is worth millions. Old boy Kilbride had them hidden right under my nose all this time, but I am smarter than he was.'

Vic inspected the bottle and noticed the inscription The Scotsman Whisky by Arthur Glasgow Master Blender, Scotland 1950. He also noticed the coat of arms similar to what he had seen in Glass's basement.

'You see Vic; this is my family's property, the last vestige of our genius at blending fine tasting whisky. The method has been passed down from my great grandfather, but it was my father who mastered the blend and now it is finally in the hands of a Glasgow, its rightful place.'

'We are finished,' announced Randy.

'Good, now burn the place to the ground,' said Glass.

Glass took up the crate holding his precious brew and he left the building followed by the rest of the robbers. He instructed Vic to use the hose from the tanker and spray the Tear Jerker on the building. Vic obeyed and the men could smell the pure scent of one hundred percent alcohol as it exited the nozzle of the hose. Meanwhile Glass went to his car, opened the trunk, and fumbled around for a bit, and then he carefully placed the crate inside. Vic put the hose back in its place on the tanker and went over to Glass to inquire if he really wanted to do this.

Glass looked at him and said, 'The first thing you should learn when committing a major crime is that you create a diversion and eliminate all traces of your presence. You have a lot to learn my son. Here, have a bottle of Scotsman and remember it is worth a lot of money, so you might want to lock it away in a safe place and have a drink of it whenever you are feeling rich.'

Vic took the bottle and placed it in the passenger seat of his vehicle, which was already stocked with other bottles of whisky. The men did not spare a space and a bottle had been placed everywhere one could fit.

'Ok, light it,' said Glass. 'See you soon and thanks for your assistance. I told you that it would be a win-win situation for all of us, well except for the late Mr. Kilbride of course. I shall be seeing you Vic and remember I am entrusting you with the Tear Jerker, so don't even think about crossing me.'

Glass sped away from the Kilbride's place as the flame started to engulf the front of the distillery. The robbers, except Vic and Tony British, ran to their respective vehicles and maneuvered quickly out of the compound. Vic and Tony British was about to follow suit when they heard barking.

'It is the dogs,' said Vic. 'We cannot leave them locked up like that; we must go and release them.'

'Maybe you cannot, but I can. Besides, the place can blow at any time and I am not risking my life for no bloody dogs' said Tony British.

Vic pointed the Taser at him and said, 'Yes you are going to risk your life for those dogs or else I am going to leave you here to burn. If I was given the choice to choose between the dogs or you, I would certainly choose to save the dogs. Now come on.'

They followed the barking and found six dogs pawing the doors of the kennel trying in vain to release themselves from their cage.

Vic said, 'Tony we have to pry these doors open, go and get that crow bar over there. Tony British hesitated, but the thought of being electrocuted or burnt to death motivated him to move quickly and he rushed for the crowbar. They could now feel the heat increasing and it would only be a matter of minutes before the place went up in a ball of fire. The men put all their strength into it and in no time they got the door open. Tony British took immediate cover, but the dogs did not care about him for they were relieved to have been freed. Vic turned to take his leave when he heard a faint bark and he turned to look where it was coming from. He discovered a baby pit-bull who seemed to have a damaged leg. Vic gathered the pup in his arms and took flight.

Tony British said, 'I will never understand you Vic Montgomery, but you are ok.'

'Thanks Tony, you are not so bad yourself' said Vic as they both fled from the building.

When they got to the front of the building they saw Harry standing beside the lorries waving at them. Vic ran past him and opened the passenger door of his vehicle and reached for the Scotsman he then reached over and took out the keys from the ignition.

Harry said, 'I noticed that you were not behind me, so I doubled back to see where you were.'

'We went back to save the dogs,' said Vic looking at Tony British. 'He then handed Harry the keys to the tanker and told him to drive it. Harry without hesitation grabbed the keys and said, 'Let us get out of here, the place looks like it is going to blow.'

The men departed in haste and they could hear the carnage that erupted as they fled the scene of the 'Great Whisky Heist'.

≍ 24 ≍

THE JOURNEY BACK

Vic *felt a little bit uneasy about* driving the tanker hauling the most valuable contraband, so that is why he decided to let Harry drive it, and he would have to take the blame if he got nicked by the Old Bills. What Vic did not know at the time was that Harry was a snitch all along. He was the one that had leaked the plans of the heist to the Italians. Vic held the pit-bull pup in his lap as he drove quickly away from the heist. He could hear the sounds of sirens heading in the directing of the great whisky heist. He looked down at the pup and then started to think about Francis. He got him off the RSPCA when he was about the same age as the little squirt that sat quietly on his lap. He said to himself *'Could this be a sign that Francis is alive and well?'* He started thinking about Glass, and he shook his head in disbelief at the diabolical plot his father in law just convinced him to carry out. There was more to Glass and he was determined to find out who the real John Glass was, not John Glass his father in law, but the man behind the mask. Who could he ask? The man was like a phantom. He was a 'do not call me I will call you' kind of bloke and Vic knew that he was going to call on him eventually. He became paranoid and he started thinking about the other men who had assisted him with the heist and wondered if their loyalty to him was still intact. His best guess was no, they had heard and seen things tonight that would make any man become possessed by the demon of greed. They will now do everything to get rich and that means double crossing whoever they could to achieve it.

Vic's thoughts drifted back to Glass and what Kilbride had said before he finished him off. *'Ask him about his daughter's death,'* Vic tried to recollect Kilbride's last words. What has Glass prevented him from revealing? He also recalled Kilbride calling Glass evil and wondered what extremes a man would really go to in the pursuit of wealth and power. *'Was Glass the aggressor acting as the victim?'* He asked himself. Since he reunited with him he saw him murdered two men in cold blood then ordered that another five be left to burn in a building. He wondered if Glass had been trailing them from the moment they left the farm. He most likely murdered the security guards at the Paisley and Dumbarton distilleries to eliminate the witnesses, but why did he warn us against hurting anybody? He knew that his main target would be at the distillery playing his weekly poker game with his workers and he used them as bait to get inside the compound. Vic tossed the questions around in his mind, but he could not think straight. He was tired and wanted to get back to London as soon as possible.

Ten miles out of Glasgow Harry, made a quick diversion down a side road leading to a dirt path. Vic saw what happened and immediately brought everyone's attention to what was going on. Randy had already seen what Harry did and he was the first to pull up. All the lorries came to a standstill and the men could see Harry's taillights dancing in the darkness. The men jump out of their vehicles and congregated by the side of the road watching Harry making his escape with the Tear Jerker.

Vic contemplated for a bit and then asked McDougal to go and fetch him the rifle. The rifle was so old and rusty and it caused him to hesitate for a while. He brought his target in focus and aimed at the tail lights as Harry tried to make his futile escape. The dirt path seemed never-ending. It was a straight one you could see down for miles.

Sam 'The Gun' McDougal assured Vic that his baby could handle the range. Vic kept his focus not knowing what would happen when he squeezed the trigger. Would it backfire? Vic asked himself. He closed his eyes and squeezed. He could hear the sound of corn popping. The entire field in the distance went up in flames. It sounded like fireworks, but it looked like a small nuclear blast. He could see the mushroom silhouette in the night-sky.

⌖ 25 ⌖

PASS THE BUCK

Even after visualizing it clearly Vic just could not take the shot. Even though the Tear Jerker could solve all his problems, he knew that it was not worth him taking the life of another man. He decided to give the shot to someone who was more distraught by the fact that Harry was escaping with hundreds of gallon of over-proof.

Vic looked around and saw McDougal licking his lips. He had not had a drink since they did the hit on the Paisley place. He was dry, thirsty and annoyed. McDougal watched the tanker in the distance as if it was a mirage depicting a lake filled with whisky. The look on his face suggested that he was very upset with the man escaping with his fare.

He grabbed the rifle from Vic and said, 'Come on young son; let me show you how it's done.'

Vic obeyed. 'I want a drink after this,' demanded McDougal. 'On the other hand, I will have that drink now.'

Randy with his annoying laugh wished he was the one with the rifle. He demanded the shot, but McDougal owned it. Tony British handed McDougal a bottle of whisky and without hesitation, he gulped down the entire bottle. He looked quenched, but that did not stop him from ordering a second bottle. He briefly savored the second bottle, unconcerned about the escaping vehicle.

The men had to bring his attention back to the matter at hand. McDougal lifted the rifle with his right hand and the second bottle of whisky with his left; he took the last gulp and dropped the bottle. He staggered a bit, composed himself and took aim as the trained marksman he claimed to be. McDougal slowly followed the lights of the vehicle, which was the only indication of its position. He gently touched the trigger and a loud bang ensued awakening the silence of the night. McDougal was nowhere in sight, but the men seemed more concerned about the fireworks. They could hear the popping of corn in the distance as the flames engulfed the fields on either side of the dirt path. The recoil had blown McDougal several meters backward from where he had been standing. He comically patted himself down as if trying to prevent himself from bursting into flames and he looked dazed. The men all laughed and McDougal himself found it amusing. He picked up his rifle, threw it over his shoulder and marched towards his truck. The men immediately realized that McDougal was getting the hell out of dodge and they too departed in haste to get as far away as possible from the site of impact. Without the suspicious looking oil tanker, the entourage now looked like regular long journey haulage lorries, nothing suspicious, just exhausted drivers.

Vic warned the remaining men not to get any smart ideas like the late Harry. There were five lorries remaining in the fleet and Vic knew he needed them all, in order to get his books up to scratch. He owed the Italians and he now owed John Glass. As a matter of fact, a big portion of the shipment belonged to Glass because the Tear Jerker alone would have brought in ten times more than what the barrels and the bottled up whisky

from the other distilleries would yield. Vic was hurt, the
Tear Jerker was sort of a gift from Glass to say don't mess
up. Glass still treated Vic like a son in law even though the
strings were no longer attached. He knew that the death
of Angie and the boys would always hang like a dark
cloud over their relationship. He knew that this was just
business for Glass, but the debt for his daughter and
grandsons would have to be repaid a thousand fold. Glass
only tolerated him out of love for his daughter as he had
only wanted to see her happy. He knew that Glass was not
a man to play games with. He was hard and serious and
his wealth and power did not come easily. He was not the
type of person you could double cross; he was very savvy
and able to detect deception a mile away.

Tonight showed Vic a more extreme side to Glass and
he wondered how he would exact his revenge on him.
After a lot of thought Vic added to his many suspicions by
wondering if Glass was using him to smuggle hard over-
proof liquor out of Scotland. The Tear Jerker could have
been doubled in volume and sold for three times its retail
price. The only problem was that it had evaporated in a
ball of fire along with a thousand acres of corn. Vic now
knew that he had an even bigger problem than the
Mussolini brothers. He felt alone and isolated because the
heist was now both personal and business, not a very
good concoction. He kept his eyes focused on the road
while his mind searched for a solution. He knew he would
have to call on old Hyde to get him out of the quandary he
was in.

⊰ 26 ⊱

STILL ON THE ROAD

The convoy was making good time. The drivers kept their feet glued to the pedals after their hasty departure from the flaming popcorn field. They started to slow down as they approached Birmingham, and decided that they would cruise at a steady speed through the city, just regular truckers making their run. The second city was fast asleep. After a mile out of the city limits, something strange happened. The front truck upon approaching an intersection immediately veered left. Vic wasn't aware of what was going on up ahead. All he could see were lorries pulling over in single file to the side of the road. The lorries had been pulled over by the Old Bill, not for inspection, but rather to prevent further congestion. There was an accident and they were only letting through small vehicles, the Lorries would have to wait. They had to close off one section of the road and the size of the Lorries would have caused further congestion up ahead.

The Officer approached the side window of the first lorry and said, 'Well mate, you may want to catch up on some sleep because it will be a long night.' The driver begged the Officer to let him through as his wife was due to have a baby. The Officer understood the driver's plight and allowed him to proceed. The lorry immediately took the first available left and disappeared. Vic could not make radio contact with the driver of the first lorry and Randy was clueless. The driver of the first lorry was Tony British.

'That slimy bastard,' barked Randy.

The men all alighted from their vehicles and congregated by the side of the road.

They were all still puzzled by what Tony British did.

Randy was still muttering under his breath. 'That bloody thief, he is so dodgy an ambulance siren would make him shit his pants.'

The men thought that Tony British was running from the Old Bill instead of escaping with the lorry filled with whisky. Tony British himself knew that he could use that along with some other fantastic story about what happened to the payload.

'Wherever he is going, he is long gone by now and we can't give chase,' said McDougal.

'Thank you for pointing that out,' said Vic sarcastically.

'Either he did a runner or he thought he would have been nicked by the Old Bill,' quietly interjected Fred, Randy's only remaining straggler.

'Well, I only hope the whisky is safe,' muttered McDougal.

'Come on lads, let's get some shut eye, we will deal with him later,' said Vic.

⋊ 27 ⋉

ROAD WORKS

The men slept for about an hour and when they woke up the road was clear, no traffic and no cops. They proceeded towards London in the early morning South East England mist. As the men approached Watford, they could see what looked like road works up ahead. By the side of the road they could see some men in high visibility jackets and hard hats holding some barriers in their hands getting ready to block the road. They looked like highway engineers out in the early morning to do their duty and they didn't seem to give the lorries a second glance.

The drivers pulled over some distance away from where they had seen the men, but as they did they noticed that up ahead two vehicles were blocking the road and they immediately thought it was an accident. Now on foot, the four men approached the vehicles blocking the road. They could not see anything as the glasses were tinted, but as they got closer they heard pistols selecting and the Mussolini brothers emerged from the Mercedes laughing.

Sergio said, 'Thank you Vic. We weren't sure you would pull it off, but you did.

I have to say, you are very smart and you have a lot of

balls.'

Silvio looked at the men and then the lorries as if he was doing a mental check.

He said, 'Wait a minute, I thought there were six lorries, but I am only counting four. What happened to the other two Vic?'

Vic said, 'One went up in a big ball of fire and the other absconded rather abruptly.

'Where is Harry?' inquired Silvio.

'He added fuel to the fire,' replied Vic

The Mussolini brothers were obviously not impressed and they both stared at Vic threateningly.

'Where is the so called 'Tear Jerker' that is what we come for?' said Silvio.

'Where is my dog?' replied Vic

'What dog?' Silvio asked.

'You sent me a note with his right ear enclosed,' said Vic.

'I don't know what you are talking about Vic. Do you know what he is talking about Sergio?'

'Nope, I haven't the slightest clue,' replied Sergio.

Silvio then said, 'As you know the deadline is close, but we decided to come and collect early before you get into London and get rid of the loot.'

The Mussolini brothers instructed their men to commandeer the lorries, but before they could retrieve the keys they heard sirens coming towards them and they quickly dashed to their vehicles.

'You owe us money Vic!' barked Sergio.

'We will be seeing you very soon,' shouted Silvio as they sped away.

The men rushed back to their lorries, but the sirens were too close for them all to pull out and drive away in time, so they stayed where they were. To their surprise, the SUV with the flashing lights drove rapidly by and took a right turn several meters up the road.

'They are definitely not after us,' said Randy over the radio.

'At least they got the Mussolini brothers off our backs,' said Vic, with a relieved tone.

⊱ PART III ⊰

THE AFTERMATH

≍ 28 ≍

BACK IN TOWN

The men entered East London at about 2pm Sunday afternoon and the streets were practically empty with only a few drunks strolling home from what seemed to have been an over extended night of partying. They headed straight to McDougal's garage which had been part of the original plan before Glass had intervened. McDougal opened the gates to his garage and looked around to see if anyone was watching. He then directed the drivers in and followed shortly behind them. He closed the gate, and once again scanned the area to see if anyone had seen them. The streets were empty except for a suspicious looking sedan they passed as they turned on to the dead end road leading to McDougal's place.

'Would you like a cup of tea?' McDougal asked the men.

'I am not staying,' said Vic. 'I am going over the pub to check on things. I will meet you back here in a few hours. Randy and Fred stay here with McDougal and keep your eyes open.'

He then went to get his car from the rear of the garage and left. He approached his pub with caution for he did not know what to expect when he opened the door. He sat in his car with the pup on his lap as he scanned the area, but did not notice anything suspicious. He then exited the vehicle, placed the pup under his jacket and crossed the street and went over to the entrance of the pub. He opened the door and silence greeted him. Everything was in place just as he left it the day before. He went upstairs to his room to check it out, and again everything was as he left it. He looked across the room and saw Francis's basket still in its usual place. He went over and gently placed the pup inside, and the dog fell asleep almost instantly. Vic was besotted with the little puppy as he reminded him so much of Francis. He pledged to take care of the dog and starting tomorrow he would visit the vet and get him to have a look at his leg and by the look of it he may have to leave him there for a few days to recover.

Vic did not know when he fell asleep, but he was awakened by a wet slimy feeling on his cheeks. He opened his eyes and found the pup licking his face.

He said, 'Hey little man, how is that leg of yours?'

The pup woofed and the sound made Vic jump. The dog had a very powerful bark. If he was not seen one would think that a fully grown dog was somewhere in the room. Vic smiled and cuddled the pup in his arms lovingly.

Vic fed the dog, took a quick shower, got dressed and headed over to McDougal's place. When he got there he found Randy and Fred fast asleep inside their lorries. He didn't disturb them as he figured that they must be very knackered and they certainly needed the rest, for the next phase of the plan would not be easy. He went to find McDougal and he found him curled up on his bed with a bottle of whisky in his hand the sight of which made Vic smile. He went over to the bed grabbed the blanket and threw it over McDougal. McDougal muttered something incoherent and went back to sleep.

Vic left the garage and returned to his pub to figure out how they were going to get the whisky off the lorries and into the basement. There was a back entrance they could use to get the whisky inside the pub and that would be the easy part. However, the difficulty was going to be getting it down the stairs and into the basement. He went to the back door and opened it. 'Perfect,' he said to himself. 'This is a blind spot; no one will see us offloading the whisky.' He then went over to the door that led to the basement and he opened, looking down at the stairs he thought about the many journeys they would have to make up and down to get the whisky hidden.

He heard what sounded like a bang on the front door and his heart skipped a beat. He became still and listened and he heard the bang again, but this time it was louder and sounded very impatient. He went to check who was calling and wondered if it was Randy coming to tell him that they were robbed. It couldn't be a punter for surely every drunkard in town knew that he couldn't water a plant. Before tonight he barely had half of bottle of whisky to serve. He didn't even have a drop of beer in the kegs. He unlocked the door and discovered Elizabeth Somerset standing there with a beautiful smile on her face.

She said, 'Hello Vic, where have you been? I called for you yesterday, but you were not in. How are you? I haven't seen you since that night and I am sorry I left you chained up, but that is the way I like to play. I have been thinking about you lately and I want to play with you some more.'

Vic looked at her with lusty eyes, but like a true detective she surveyed the room and noticed an open door at the back of the pub.

She said, 'I didn't know you have a door back there.

Can I have a look?'

Without waiting for an answer she walked passed Vic and headed for the door.

'It is just the back of the pub, nothing to see there,' said Vic following quickly behind.

As she approached the back door she noticed another opened door. 'Where does that one lead?' she asked pointing in the direction of the basement.

'That's the basement,' replied Vic.

'What do you keep there?' she inquired.

'I don't use it much,' said Vic. 'The previous owner used it to store his old stuff, some very strange items I might add. The bloke who owned this pub acquired a lot of things from his many travels around the world.'

'I want to have a look,' said Elizabeth with excitement in her voice.

'They're just some old stuff that I am planning on flogging to see if I can get this pub up and running again.'

Elizabeth was now keener on visiting the basement and she begged Vic to take her there. Vic yielded to her persistence and he went behind the bar and grabbed a huge torch.

He said, 'Come on lets go, but only for a quick look. My dog is still missing and I have to go out and find him.'

Vic led the way and Elizabeth followed closely behind holding on to his shirt.

'Where are the lights?' she asked.

'The genius who installed the electricity placed it at the bottom of the stairs.'

They reached the bottom and Vic flipped the light switch and the place was now illuminated revealing a tunnel that opened up to the right.

'What was this place used for?' she asked.

'I am not sure,' replied Vic cautiously.

'It feels like a bunker down here,' she said staring at

the roof of the tunnel. She then turned to him and said, 'This is a very interesting place and I cannot wait to see the rest of it. Go on lead the way.'

Vic led the way and Elizabeth took her time as she basked in the fact that she was entering a place that not many people knew existed. They reached the opening to a large cavern and he pointed to the place where the antiques were stored.

He said, 'There they are, I am guessing that they have been here for over a hundred years.'

'I cannot believe you allowed the pub to run out of business when you have these treasures stashed away down here,' she said. She then went over took up a lamp and inspected it closely. She brushed some dust off to reveal an inscription on the base if the lamp. It read, A Creation by Thomas Edison, by Order of His Majesty the King.

She said, 'This lamp must be worth thousands of pounds, even more if it works.

'I didn't want to touch the old man's stuff and for all I know they could be cursed. The whole bloody place seems to be cursed,' said Vic

'Why so superstitious?' asked Elizabeth.

Vic did not answer the question, but it got him thinking that maybe he was cursed indeed. Elizabeth seemed to have read his thoughts and she looked at him and said, 'I think you are the one who is cursed, crazy even, but for some reason you fascinate me. I know you have had a hard life with the death of your family, prison and the spell in that mental asylum, but I am amazed that you are still able to carry on a normal life. Well not exactly normal, but you seem to get by.'

She saw that his eyes were now filled with water and she quickly changed the subject. She shifted her attention from him, so that he could dry his eyes. Her eyes caught a large flat square object that was propped up against a wall. She took the torch and went over to investigate and noticed that the object was wrapped with a silk fabric. She carefully removed the fabric from the object and underneath she discovered a painting.

'Do you know what this is?' she asked.

Vic went over and said, 'Yes, it's a painting. What?'

'This is not just a painting,' she said. 'This is a Rembrandt and if my memory serves me right, this painting was stolen from the British Museum in the 1960s, and was never to be seen again. The heist was not made public and after several years of searching for the painting the museum commissioned the best artist at the time to create a replica and over the years the theft became a myth and now the fake copy has been accepted as the original. They did that intentionally, so that the original could never be sold and whoever had stolen it was left with a worthless original painting. The museum, however, did not give up their quest to find the painting and they would pay millions for its return.'

Vic took back the torch from Elizabeth and he looked at the painting with interest. He then asked, 'What is the title of the painting and what does it mean? What story does it tell?'

Elizabeth replied and said, 'The painting is called 'The Return of the Prodigal Son'. This painting was one of Rembrandt's last works before he died and as such it became the most coveted. If you were paying attention at Sunday school like a good little boy you would have been able to identify the story just by looking at it. It was a long time since I have heard the story, but if my memory serves me right, the Prodigal Son was a coming of age young man who wanted to be independent. Tired of his boring existence living on a farm he demanded his inheritance and decided to leave home and go out and explore the world. His parents gave him his inheritance and they bid him farewell. He had a brother who at the same time was given his inheritance as well, but he decided to stay and help his parents. The prodigal son vowed never to return home until he was wealthy. However, he quickly squandered his inheritance and became destitute. He was literally starving and he who once had many servants to command became a servant. After years of abject poverty he decided to return home and begged his father's forgiveness.'

'Did his father forgive him?' asked Vic.

Elizabeth replied, 'Yes, he did as a matter of fact the father instructed his servants to fetch the finest robe and kill the fattest cow in the pasture for there would be a feast to celebrate the return of his son. When the brother heard of his arrival he became very angry and refused to attend the feast for he had stayed behind and labored for his father while his lazy brother went out in the world and made nothing of himself. In other words, he was really pissed.'

'But what is the meaning of the story?' Vic asked.

She replied, 'The Prodigal Son discovered that it was much better to work by his father's side rather than at the mercy of strangers and slave drivers. He also discovered that life on the farm wasn't too bad after all.'

'That was a very fascinating story. I must read it sometime,' said Vic.

She said, 'Yes, it is a very interesting story and there are many Prodigal Sons around today.'

Vic then said, 'I am certainly not a prodigal son for I never knew my father. Anyway, it is getting rather late, so I will have to give you an extended tour of the place another time. Come, let us go now.'

⊰ 29 ⊱

THE BEST EVER

As Vic turned away from the painting his hands slightly rubbed against her breasts. He looked in her eyes and they were filled with lust and passion. Before he could speak she pressed her lips against his and he did not hesitate to push his tongue deep inside her mouth. She held on to it with tight lips and did not let go until she could taste his blood inside her mouth. He felt angry at the pain she had caused him, but he did not react negatively, instead he held on to her tongue as she did his and sucked on it until she pushed him away. Once freed from the grip of his lips on her tongue, she attacked him again with increased passion. She jumped on him and lapped her legs around his waist, and then went to work on his neck.

The sensation of her tongue on his neck gave him goose bumps, and he liked it. She blew softly in his ear and then whispered, 'I want you Vic, ever since that night I have been thinking about you inside me and how good it made me feel. It was probably the best I have ever had and I have had a few.'

Vic secured the torch and then he unhooked her bra then pinned her up against the wall. She kissed him again, but this time delicately. He braced her against the wall with his thighs and then he used his hands to remove her laced thong. She gasped as he made the first thrust inside her and wrapped her arms around his neck and squeezed. The more she squeezed the deeper he penetrated her. She trembled as she erupted on his blade.

'More! Give me more!' she screamed.

He obliged her and she came over and over again. She was like a blocked dam long awaiting a hammer to break down the walls so that her water could flow freely. She tried to push him off, but he wasn't finished with her, for he had also long awaited release. Still inside her, he spun her around and placed her on an old table that a few seconds before was covered with books. He lifted her skirt higher, so that he could feel her skin against his as he penetrated her. She was on the verge of bursting again and he increased his circular motion, so that he could join her this time. She caught his rhythm and started to gyrate underneath him. His body became rigid and his toes curled in his boots as he was about to erupt. The tension eased as he collided with her and she turned, smiled and kissed him on the cheek.

She said, 'I told you Victor Montgomery that you are the best I have ever had and from this I can say that you are certainly not a one hit wonder.'

Vic could not speak for he was still trying to catch his breath. She laughed and reached for the torch. 'Where did you put my undies?' she asked shining the torch around the room.

'I think I threw them somewhere behind me,' replied Vic

'I don't see it,' said Elizabeth. 'I will just have to leave it down here to be a part of antiquity.' They both laughed as Elizabeth led the way out of the room.

She said, 'This has got to be the strangest place I have

ever had sex. I feel like I was transported back into the past. I have never cum so many times.'

Vic was pleased with himself and he said, 'we should do this more often.'

Elizabeth replied, 'I don't think that is a good idea. I shouldn't even be doing this with you; after all you are a main suspect in the killing of Big Mike and his cousins.'

Vic said, 'I told you I have nothing to do with that. Yes, I knew the bloke and yes I knew that he came to London to seek revenge, but I had nothing to do with the murder.'

'Well, you are still a favorite for the killing, so I suggest you tread very carefully,' she turned to him and said as they reached the staircase.

As Elizabeth started to climb the staircase, Vic eyes caught her bare ass and he immediately became hard again. He held on to her waist then moved his hand up to find one firm, round breast. Caressing her nipple slowly and she became wet. Vic already had his trousers down and she searched for his manhood. She found it and slowly guided it through the darkness to find her already moistened pasture. He used her water to wet the tip of his manhood, so that it could effortlessly glide into her. He gave it to her slowly this time and she matched his rhythm with precision. And he remained in that position until he ejaculated. She enjoyed the warmth of his cum inside her and she used her body to milk every last drop from his manhood. Vic was still hard and he wanted more.

He enjoyed her body and he has never felt so good making love to another woman except for his wife. She continued to gyrate on him encouraging him to remain hard for she too wanted more. He was back in his rhythm, but was immediately thrown off when the dog barked.

'What is that?' she asked.

He ejected himself from her, pulled up his trousers

and said, 'It is a little pup that I have rescued from the RSPCA. He is a cute little squirt.'

'I want to see him,' said Elizabeth excitedly.

Elizabeth immediately fell in love with the pit bull pup. 'He is a cute little bugger. It amazes me how something so cute can grow up to be so vile,' she said looking at Vic.

She noticed that the pup had an injured leg and she asked him what happened. He concocted some cock and bull story and she bought it.

'I am thinking about taking him to see the vet in the morning, but I have so much to do here. I have been thinking about what you said down in the basement and I am going to flog some of the antiques and use the money to renovate the pub. I am sure that Patrick Carlisle will not be turning in his grave or his grandson Peter wherever that bloke is, would not be too upset if I use the money to fix up the place. I may even give it back its old name The Refuge.'

Elizabeth said, 'I am free tomorrow, so I could take the pup to see the vet if you like. I can even take him off your hands right now, so that you can start your plans for the renovations. I will bring him back to you when he is healed.'

Vic said 'Ok, thank you Elizabeth, I appreciate your help.'

She smiled and kissed him and said, 'Thank you for tonight, it is always a pleasure.' She then kissed him again and left with the pup cuddled under her arms.

⋈ 30 ⋈

OFFLOAD THE LOOT

It *was about 10pm when Vic* returned to McDougal's Garage. It would be hard work to get all the whisky from the lorries and into the basement. He could do with more manpower and wished that Harry hadn't evaporated with the Tear Jerker and Tony British didn't do a runner. He found the three men up and alert playing a heated game of dominoes.

'Do you have anything here to eat Sam?' Vic asked. 'I am starving, I haven't had anything to eat since we left Glass's farm and I have just done some serious work down in the basement.'

McDougal replied, 'Yes, there is some food in the kitchen?' He then slammed his last domino on the table and laughed and said, 'I won, so that's ten bottles of whisky for me.'

'What are you doing?' asked Vic sternly.

'We are playing dominoes, obviously. And we are using our share of the whisky for the stakes' said Fred sarcastically.

Vic shot him a serious look and he did not say anything else. McDougal at the same time was walking away with his winnings when Vic caught him by the arm and pulled him back.

He said, 'This is not a game McDougal. These bottles must never be seen again. We are going to hide every last bottle of whisky on those four lorries.'

McDougal freed himself from Vic's hands and said, 'Where have you been? We have been sitting around here all night waiting for you and I am starting to feel like an old mug.'

'Calm down McDougal,' said Vic. 'I was at the pub preparing the place for the bottles.'

'And that took you all evening and night?' Randy interjected.

'Yes it bloody took me all evening and night,' barked Vic.

'Why are you being so defensive Vic? Is there something you are not telling us?' asked Randy.

'Aright, Detective Elizabeth Somerset paid me a visit.'

'Interesting, so she had you all evening and night,' said Randy laughing.

'I don't trust that girl,' said McDougal. 'Hell, I don't trust any copper. Did she by any chance mention her partner?' he asked.

'No, she didn't. Come to think of it, I find that a bit strange,' replied Vic.

'I guess you were too hard in the head to think of it then,' said Randy and everybody laughed.

'McDougal is right. I don't trust her either. She has a partner, excuse me, had a partner, but yet she always seems to be working on her own, which I find very peculiar.'

'I have been thinking about that,' said Vic. 'She always seems to turn up suddenly. I think she has been watching me ever since the Big Mike affair.'

'Do you think she knows about the whisky heist?' asked McDougal.

'Even if she did I got no indication of that, so she either doesn't know or she is a brilliant actress. Furthermore, she was more interested in the lamps and paintings down in the old basement,' replied Vic.

'You brought her to the basement?' asked a surprised Randy. 'Do you mean the same basement where we are planning to stash the loot?'

'Yes,' replied Vic with his head down.

'Unbelievable,' said Randy. 'She knows! We are all going to be nicked I tell you.'

Vic said, 'Don't be paranoid Randy. She discovered the basement by chance. She saw the door to the back of the pub open and she went to have a look outside and that's when she noticed the door to the basement. How could she possibly know about the heist from merely visiting an old basement?'

'Anything is possible,' replied Randy. 'And I think it is best if we don't trust anyone from now on.'

'What is the plan to offload the whisky and get them safely in the basement without being seen?' asked McDougal.

'We will have to do it tonight,' said Vic. 'Let me eat and think about it.'

He then left the men and went towards McDougal's kitchen to find food. McDougal placed the whisky that he had won from the domino game back on to the lorry and returned to his seat.

He looked at Randy and said, 'I don't feel too good about this. Something doesn't smell right. I cannot put my hands on it, but I think more is going on here than we can conceive.'

Randy said, 'What scares me is that the beautiful detective has our friend Vic under a love spell and he is going to get sloppy.'

Vic returned with a bowl filled to the brim with the

food McDougal had prepared. He said, 'This is delicious McDougal, I didn't know you could cook so well. If I had you cooking for the punters at the pub maybe I would still be in business. You could have been less generous with the whisky sauce though, but it is palatable.'

He grabbed a chair and joined them at the table and said, 'Gentlemen, it has been a hell of a ride and I am happy we are back here safely. Even though we have been double-crossed by two of our comrades, I am happy that we still have four lorries filled to the brim with good Scottish whisky. I am asking you to be patient while we find a buyer and get it as far away from us as possible and then we will share the money.'

Fred was not exactly pleased with the fact that he had to wait before he got paid and he was expecting his money tonight, at least that was what Randy had promised him.

'I don't care about the whisky. I want my money now!' Fred demanded.

'Have you been listening to anything that I have just said?' asked Vic sternly.

'I was promised that I would have been paid after the job. Not a month after, but tonight, right now!' shouted Fred.

Vic looked at Randy and said, 'You brought him in so he is your responsibility. Pay him and send him on his way, I don't ever want to see his face again.'

Randy realized that Vic was very serious and he spotted the familiar rage in his friend's eyes. He had seen it many times before when they were in Pentonville and the last time he saw it was when they were dealing with the almost forgotten Peter Carlisle.

Randy said, 'Come with me Fred. I have some money back at my place.'

He asked Vic to lend him his car and Vic quickly threw

him the keys. When Randy reached the car he grabbed Fred by the throat and pinned him up against it.

He said, 'Are you trying to get us both killed you bloody fool?' He released his grip as Fred was about to pass out, and he slapped him a couple times across the face. 'Get in the car you greedy bastard!'

Fred obeyed and went to sit in the passenger seat without saying anything and he kept his mouth shut for most of the journey.

'You cannot play around with Vic like that. You don't know the guy, hell, I have known him for years and I still cannot read him. He is unpredictable and I am certain he was about to kill you back there.'

'I am not afraid of him,' said Fred. 'Why don't we just kill him and the old man and keep the whisky for ourselves? I have no loyalty to none of them, only you.'

Randy looked over at Fred and laughed hysterically. He said, 'You don't have the balls to stand up to Vic Montgomery.'

I don't have to stand up to him a bullet from behind will take care of that,' said Fred looking over at Randy. 'Every man for himself, Tony British was smart he took his payment straight up as he did not intend on sitting around waiting for an entire month. If I wanted to be paid monthly I would have been holding down a regular nine to five. We are both criminals and criminals are opportunists, so I don't accept that patience bollocks.'

'Every man for himself indeed,' agreed Randy.

'I am happy you are seeing things my way,' said Fred.

Randy accelerated the vehicle, and he quickly put on his seat belt and braced himself. Before Fred realized what was happening Randy pressed hard on the brakes which sent Fred flying through the wind screen. Randy did not stop but drove straight over him. He could hear the crack of the bones as the wheels passed over Fred's already dead body. He then reversed, popped the trunk and placed Fred's mangled body inside. He went back in the vehicle, flung it around and headed back to McDougal's garage.

Meanwhile at the garage Vic and McDougal was discussing the plan to offload the loot.

Vic said, 'We will have to get rid of these lorries. No way can we drive any of these up to the pub without looking suspicious. That Tesco lorry over there is a dead giveaway for anybody saw it pulling up to a pub in the dead of the night would figure out that something dodgy was going on.'

'Yes, I agree. We need something less conspicuous,' said McDougal. 'The white lorry doesn't look too suspect, so we can use it to transport the whisky from here over to the pub. It will take us all night, but it will not look too suspicious.'

Randy returned and Vic and McDougal were surprised to see him back so soon. He handed back Vic his keys and saw that Vic noticed his bloodied hands.

He said, 'I am sorry Vic, but there was an accident and your car will need some repairs, but nothing McDougal cannot fix.'

'Where is my car?' demanded Vic.

'I parked it back there where I found it earlier,' replied Randy.

'Come with me,' said Vic.

The men all headed to where the car was parked and Vic saw the broken windscreen in the distance.

He asked, 'Where is Fred?'

Randy replied, 'There was a fox in the road and I had to brake suddenly to avoid hitting it. Poor old Fred wasn't wearing his seatbelt and he flew straight through the windscreen.'

'Where is he now?' asked McDougal.

'I scraped him up off the road and placed him in the trunk,' answered Randy.

Vic opened the trunk and almost threw up what he had eaten earlier. He then looked at Randy curiously and said, 'Haven't you ever heard of DNA you bloody idiot?' Randy looked puzzled, but he did not reply to Vic's question.

Vic looked at McDougal and said, 'We will have to get rid of the body and destroy the car.'

'We can crush it with the body in it,' said McDougal. 'No one will notice that a body is inside and furthermore, this is a junk yard so there is no need to move it anywhere.'

'Ok,' said Vic looking at Randy. 'We will deal with it after we offload the whisky and you are going to do most of the work.'

The three men worked tirelessly throughout the night offloading and transporting the whisky to the pub. They drove the lorry up around the back of the pub, which was hidden from view by a large office building which also hid the docks that lay on the other side. The men carried the crates and boxes through the back of the pub and down in the basement to the area Vic had prepared. They made many trips and after several hours all the whisky was safely stored.

The whisky was now safely sitting in its temporary resting place. The task now was to protect it and look for a buyer they could trust. They would have to keep an eye out for the likes of Tony British and the Mussolini brothers. As far as Vic could tell, they were the only blokes in London who knew about the heist and he was expecting them. He wished he had Francis to guard the place for he knew that no one dared trespass when he was around, but he wasn't and all he had was Randy and Sam 'The Gun' McDougal. He wondered if he should strike the Mussolini brothers before they came to pay him a visit. He knew that the next encounter with the brothers may be his last and his best chance of surviving was to catch them off guard. He asked McDougal to prepare some pistols and he advised him and Randy to start carrying weapons also.

⊰ 31 ⊱

THE BIG HIT

The hit on the Mussolini brothers was never going to be easy. They lived in a fortress and were very mindful of the places they visited twice. Only after a long period of time they would return and they usually turned up unannounced. If they were scheduling a meeting the venue would be changed at the last minute. This would throw off the rivals who were just waiting for the best moment to strike. The brothers had survived by following this principle. They were like professional poker players and you could never read their faces.

Vic's world was caving in. He had to get rid of them before they could get to him. He didn't have many places to seek refuge, so they always had the advantage. He was at their mercy, they just had to say the word and he would get caught in their web. The Mussolini brothers controlled East London and even a whisper of dissent could get a man killed. They had eyes and ears everywhere.

Everyone sings for the right price. Most of the informers never got past the rehearsal for if you were a new chirper, you would be vetted and tested. You had better bring the goods and you sure as hell better be able to bring useable information. If you were proven to be unreliable then you would go 'swimming with the fishes' as they liked to put it. If you were proven to be reliable then you would be rewarded with a small position within the organization, which was a huge achievement, because no one could get in easily, especially if you were an unknown. Once you got in, whether at entry level or not, you would have access to fancy suits, cars, women and money. You would have open access, but you would be owned.

The Mussolini brothers were the largest employers in town, albeit it, unbeknownst to the treasury. They had a hand in every field of enterprise. Surely they had some serious competitors; this is East London we are talking about. There were other ruthless gangsters in town, but they had to keep quiet. They were outnumbered and outclassed. They not only had to conceal their activities from the law, they also had to keep things quiet from the Mussolini brothers. If the brothers knew exactly how much they were raking in, then they would be taxed at a rate double the amount the government would charge. It would prove more profitable if they went legit and paid their taxes like other law abiding citizens. They all wanted to get rid of the Mussolini brothers, but nobody had the balls. Many tried and failed and many lives were lost because the brothers were always one step ahead.

Vic was now determined to do himself and everyone in East London a favor, the job was his, he deserved it. He was determined to get them one way or another, even if he got nicked after. It would have to be a quiet job, no one must have a clue, and he would be the mysterious hero who saved East London from the wretched brothers. There would be many rumors, only rumors. Randy would be the only accomplice, and Vic was confident that he could keep his mouth shut; after all, he would be implicated if he chirped. The pistol he got from McDougal would be perfect for the job; it could get it done effectively. The silencer would ensure that the execution was quietly done, but Vic wanted to hear them scream. He knew that for the job to be squeaky clean, he would have to abduct them like they did Francis. But how would this be possible? They had a twenty four hour security team that was impenetrable. The mission would have to be stealthy, perfectly coordinated at the right place and the right time. There must be a loophole, a window, they must have vulnerabilities. Get them out of the equation and he would have rid himself of his biggest headache since Big Mike. Even though he still pondered about what had happened to Mike and his cousins, he was grateful for the favor. The other men he owed money were civilized enough to understand reason, but the brothers took the phrase 'Deadline' literally, nothing gets overdue. Everything must be paid on time and paid in full, that was their word and they stuck to it. Vic knew that the brothers would not be satisfied with only the money he owed them. They knew about the heist and they had seen the lorries and Vic was certain that they wanted the whisky, so he had to act now. He called up Randy, and they met and schemed.

Interestingly, the Mussolini brothers stopped by the pub a few days later and even though Vic and Randy were surprised to see them, they kept their cool. There was something strangely different because the brothers came in alone. They seemed unconcerned about security; it was as if they owned the bloody place. They went over to where Vic and Randy were sitting. Without acknowledging them, the brothers started to talk, consecutively, as if they had previously planned what they were about to say.

'You know Vic, we could use a guy like you in our

organization, but you are a bit on the sly side. We would not be able to trust you. Besides, you seem to be doing alright by yourself pulling off that whisky heist and all, the only problem is you don't like to pay your taxes and we don't like that. As a matter of fact, it drives us crazy.'

They continued, 'Would you like a drink Vic? This will be our place soon, whether you can pay your debt or not. Besides we are certain you won't be able to pay. We are no longer playing with you Vic, no more cat and mouse games, you have eaten your last cheese. No more, no excuses, you have nothing, we own you. We only kept you two alive, so you could do your little whisky heist while we sit back and wait. Now, where is the whisky?'

'It's in the back,' announced Randy promptly.

Vic looked at him in astonishment. 'Well go on! Fetch the torch and show them the bloody way then,' said Vic.

The men escorted the brothers to the basement. It had a damp and moldy smell and the air in the passageway leading to the entrance of the storage area was stifling. Vic did not turn on the lights as he did not want the brothers to see all that was in the basement. It took the Mussolini brothers a while to adjust their lungs to the foreign environment. Their expensive Italian suits would most certainly not survive the journey and they reached that conclusion when they heard the distant squeaks. They both look at each other and then continued to follow Vic and Randy like a SWAT team would. They were now entering dark territory. The light from the torch illuminated the way and the darkness disappeared before them. The brothers were extremely careful; and followed with their guns drawn.

The squeaking became louder and Randy shone the torch ahead to get a view of what awaited them ahead and then they saw...There were rats everywhere, the place was infested! Vic figured that they must have disturbed them when they were storing the whisky, for there had been no signs of rats a few days earlier. *'Where the hell they came from?'* he thought. The men could hear the rats succumbing to the wrath of the soles of their shoes as they were unable to avoid crushing the little critters. The Mussolini brothers felt disgust rather than pity for the innocent creatures. The stillness of the basement became alive with squealing and rustling as the rats tried to make their escape with nowhere to go. Randy lifted the torch and noticed that they were trying to escape through a small hole, all fighting to squeeze through at the same time. The Mussolini brothers had to expel a couple pellets to scare them off, for not all the rats were running away. Some were hungry and fearless. Even the big brave Randy got the chills when the light made contact with their eyes; they were blood red with hunger and even seemed angry about the disturbance. It felt like a scene in a Dracula movie, luckily these rats couldn't fly. Some of them were only skin and bones, looking very skeletal. While others were almost as big as cats and looked very well fed and those were the ones that kept coming.

'Holy shit!' said Randy when he saw a Godzilla looking creature coming his way. He instinctively put the torch in front of his face at the right time as the animal came in for the kill. The pain must have been excruciating, the noise did not sound like that of a rat but that of a bear as it was engulfed in flames. The smaller rats descended upon the still steaming carcass and ravaged it within seconds. The men realized that these vermin meant business and grabbed for anything they could find to keep the hungry monsters at bay. They were successful and they made their way safely to the room where the whisky was stored.

Patrick Carlisle had used the basement back in the

day to store his most valuable merchandise and stolen contraband. This section of the basement was intact, just as it was when The Refuge was still in operation. The dusty barrels and chests told of a past of voyages and adventure for Mr. Carlisle. The barrels lined the cavernous dungeon and the labels chiseled into their sides told of their origin. Jamaican spiced rum from Port Royal and moonshine from New Orleans. Persian carpets wrapped up in their misery and dismay of being confined to that dark place never to grace the glistening floors of palaces and stately homes. They wasted in the dark, choked by their own beauty and splendor. Patrick Carlisle had ventured far and wide. He walked the streets and climbed the mountains and traversed the valleys of many foreign lands taking back whatever his ships could carry. The place was haunted by memories longing to be relived and stories wanting to be heard.

Vic rarely ventured there, the place gave him the creeps, but it was the only place he could hide that amount of whisky without all the boozers in town knowing about it, for they would have raided the place the same night it came in. Vic knew that his newly discovered tenants could not chew through glass, so they were not a problem.

The men entered a large room and proceeded with caution. After the episode with the rats they were extra careful and even though Vic and Randy had visited the place a couple days before, they were still not sure what to expect. The place was littered with antiques, but the brothers were only interested in the brew. Sergio snatched the torch from Randy's hand and started to look around the room. Their eyes lit up when they spotted the bottle of Scotsman. They rushed over and picked it up. They inspected the bottle and both said in awe, 'The rarest whisky in the world, the Scotsman.' Vic had forgotten all about the Scotsman and was not happy that the Mussolini brothers found it.

Sergio looked at Vic and said, 'Do you know what this is? This bottle is worth ten times more than all the whisky you have in here. Only the lips of the worthy could taste the pure perfection of the brewer's hands.'

The brothers obviously felt that they were worthy; for they opened the bottle and both took a drink. It was as if they melted away into a state of calmness, you could see the satisfaction on their faces.

'Only a few are worthy to taste this perfection,' they said again turning to face Vic and Randy.

The brothers started to look uncomfortable, they were still talking, but the words were becoming incoherent and they staggered and fell. Vic and Randy could not believe what they were seeing; it was as if they had witnessed a miracle. They could not believe their luck. Vic immediately surmised that the bottle must have been meant for him for no one, including him could resist a taste of the legendary Scotsman not after the history lesson from Glass who he had witnessed killing a man in cold blood over it. He knew for certain that he would have definitely indulged sooner or later.

'Why would Glass contaminate a priceless bottle of brew?' he asked although the question was not directed to anyone in particular.

'Unless it is not the real thing and those two geniuses couldn't tell the difference,' said Randy after which his annoying laugh ensued.

'Good things come to those who are patient,' said Vic.

'I am sure Glass had something to do with this, that bastard, now we will have to test every bottle.'

Vic had a plan, the place was overflowing with rats, and they were potential test subjects. There were at least ten rats available to test each bottle. There were also enough available to properly dispose of the Mussolini brothers without a trace. The men moved the bodies from the room and transferred them to another part of the basement. They let in a couple hundred diners after which they sealed it off with the Mussolini brothers inside. They would disappear into oblivion and Vic didn't even have to get his hands dirty.

'I didn't even get a chance to ask them about Francis again; those greedy bastards,' a disappointed Vic muttered to himself.

⚹ **32** ⚹

THE TUNNEL

As *the men made their departure* from the tomb they *could* hear the commotion over the buffet they had left behind. You could literally hear them fighting, each trying to find a spot on the platter to nibble away. They made their way back through the gauntlet of killer rats swiftly but cautiously. They arrived at the spot where Godzilla and his pals had attacked them, but it was quiet and rat free. It must have taken them a good while to all get through the hole in the ceiling that Randy had discovered, but they were all gone. When they reached the hole in the ceiling Vic felt a light breeze on the back of his neck. He wondered how on earth could there be fresh air coming through when the ceiling was nothing but the floor of the pub, or so he thought. He scanned the ceiling carefully, then he examined the walls, but it looked as though they were built to last for an eternity. Before Patrick Carlisle acquired the place it had already existed for centuries. The tunnel itself felt like a bunker, and Vic was almost certain that it had been used as a place of protection in times of wars or whatever crusades had been taking place during the time of its erection.

A thought came to him that brought a smile to his

face. He approached the wall to the right of the stairs leading back to the pub, and he caressed it for a moment. He placed an ear next to it, but could hear nothing. He tapped it with his index finger, but still could not tell whether the wall was hollow or not. He still had a strong notion that it was a trick wall, a secret refuge, a panic room perhaps. He searched for cracks and crevices or a loose brick that when triggered would open the wall and reveal a room filled with wonderful treasures of old. He was now eager to discover what was on the other side. He scanned the area and saw a brick lying in the corner of the passage. He went over, picked it up and held it firm. The brick partially crumbled as it made contact with the wall. It did not totally disintegrate and upon contact with the wall he could hear the hollow sound he was anticipating, which suggested that the wall was not as solid as it seemed. There was now a small crack that gave him a slight view of the other side. It was a trick wall indeed as the material used in its construction was very thin. Vic thought to himself that it must have been used for long term storage and it had obviously not been disturbed since its erection. He instructed Randy to fetch the sledge hammer from behind the bar and bring more lighting. He also told him to bring a weapon, anything he could lay his hands on because he wasn't sure what manner of creatures lay in wait on the other side. He tried not to think about the possibility of snakes because he hated them, and they made him cringe. What he hated most of all was their eyes and the evil stare they have when they are just about to strike their prey. With this thought, he further instructed Randy to fetch the oven lighter and one of his cheap body sprays. Wondering what the hell Vic was on about, Randy obeyed.

Vic now realized that his palm was badly bruised and was now feeling the effect of the brick on brick collision.

The hard material remaining in his hand after the contact caused the joints in his fingers to hurt. He pushed the damaged hand in his pocket as soon as he heard Randy returning, and all outward show of the pain vanished as soon as they made face to face contact as he knew that Randy would take the Mick if he noticed that he was crying over a little pain caused by a thousand year old brick. He secured the oven lighter and body spray. Armed and ready, he instructed Randy to hit the wall with the sledge hammer, as hard as his heavy-set body would allow. Randy responded with his usual hyena sounding laugh and without hesitation smashed the sledge hammer against the wall. Without any resistance the wall caved in and revealed a tunnel on the other side. Vic's excitement and interest grew even stronger, he felt like an archaeologist discovering a Pharaoh's tomb.

From the torch light they could see what looked like a narrow rail track and to Vic's relief there were no signs of snakes or any other critters so far. They could make out other tunnels, but those did not have any rail tracks, so they decided to follow the one that did and proceeded straight ahead. This would guide them in a straight line so they would not make a foray into a maze. As they proceeded down the dark track, they could see what looked like the remains of medieval scaffolding and construction. The walls on either side of the tunnel were chiseled in a manner that made it obvious that they were trotting down the path of a very old mining shaft. They continued to follow the tracks for about a mile and even though they grew tired, they kept going, eager to find out what was at the end of the tunnel. They finally reached the end where they found three large metal carts on the tracks. They surmised that the containers must have been used to haul out dirt. Vic tried to move one, but his effort proved futile. Randy also gave it a try, but it did not budge. They both reckoned that the tracks would need to be greased if they were ever planning on moving the carts. Vic was not keen on trekking the mile back to the wall, and he intended to use the container for transport.

The end of the track was blocked with what looked like oak. Centuries of wear and tear had caused it to rot and it had lost all its firmness. Even Vic himself could break through with perfect ease. He barely made contact and the obstruction gave way. The sunlight came pouring in followed by a strong smell of fish. Both men looked at each other with the same expression on their faces. They now had an answer to their biggest problem since Big Mike and the most recent Mussolini brothers.

Before the newly discovered tunnel, the men had no idea how they would remove the whisky from the basement once they had found a buyer and they dreaded repeating the laborious task they had carried out a couple days before. Getting it in was the easy part, it looked like any other delivery, but getting it out would draw suspicion. Vic barely had enough to keep his punters watered; therefore, it would be strange for him to be selling the stuff wholesale. Furthermore, whisky only exits a pub in the bellies of the patrons or through the drainage pipes of the loo. The most difficult part of getting rid of the booze is that there would be many wandering eyes in town and surely word about the heist must have already been spreading throughout the land. It was compounded by the fact that they had just robbed some of the most dangerous and influential men in Scotland, thanks to Glass.

Glass' willing assistance left a bad taste in Vic's mouth. He still didn't know if it was a coincidence or if Glass had been expecting him. Glass' calm reaction upon seeing him made Vic uneasy for he now knew that his father-in-law was a very serious man who laid traps and dangled carrots as a means of exacting his revenge on those who double-crossed him. Vic had previous knowledge about it as even Angie had feared her father and his irrational actions.

Vic decided to stop thinking about Glass and start planning a way out of the never-ending struggles of his life. As soon as he paid one debt then another arose to take its place. It was like a continuous saga and he wished for the day when it would be over, whether by death or redemption.

Vic also decided that he would get James Johnston to come in and test the bottles to ensure that they were not all laced with poison. The bottles would then be washed out and stripped of their original labels. The spirit would then be rebottled and ready to bear the label of a dodgy distributor. The plan was to get an exporter to relieve him of the loot. He would have to go wholesale demanding payment up front and for this he would have to give the lucky exporter a large discount. He could not approach anyone honest for it would be quite evident that the whisky was stolen. Which brewer wouldn't be happy to advertise his brand? Unless Vic could come up with his own brand, register it and formally enter the whisky trade. Unfortunately that would be a little too honest for him. He knew that with honesty came Her Majesty's Revenues and Customs and the hawkish regulators. The regulators would be breathing down his neck, especially in the booze business. The government has always had a history of interfering with the trade under the guise of curbing binge- drinking. The reality was that, the taxman taxed everyone involved, from the barley farmers to the brewer right down to the bloke that supplies the tumblers to the pub owner. These taxes and regulations are good for the criminals; all they had to do was to price their products just below the government's tax line. The blokes who sold the fake stuff could lower their prices even more without affecting their huge profit margins. However, they themselves had to track the government regulated prices and sell some of their liquor within the same bracket or else it would be obvious to the consumers that the quality was inferior. Vic arrived at the conclusion that he would be better off staying underground, especially owing to the fact that he did not own a distillery. He could barely afford to stock his own pub, much less go into the wholesale business over night. The stock tucked away in the basement was worth a hefty sum, and if he could shift it all in one go, then that would take care of all his financial problems and the tunnel provided him with the answer.

The men surveyed the outside of the tunnel and realized that it was in close proximity to the docks. They were confused about their exact location and it felt as if they were on the other side of town. They could not see the pub; the view was blocked by large waterfront apartments and office buildings. They turned the corner of the last building and saw the pub in the distance.

The pub looked decadent in comparison to everything around it. It was like a relic nestled between modern architecture. Vic was lucky to still have the license to operate the pub for it was a protected building. It stood as a testament of the skill employed by the earlier builders who made the structure to last for eternity. The place must have been renovated over a hundred times, however all the previous owners took care in maintaining its ancient appearance and décor. All materials for renovating the place had to look exactly like the original. If Vic wanted to change a bulb in the 16th century chandeliers he had to inform the blokes at the heritage trust and get their permission beforehand. Furthermore, he couldn't just buy any light bulb from his neighborhood off license. They had to be made by some old geezers who specialized in ancient glassware.

Many attempts had been made to acquire the pub from Vic by unsavory characters, including those from museum trusts. These guys were the most dangerous because they could take away your property forcefully, but legally. When dealing with the guys on the other side of the street you could crack a few skulls to dissuade them from trying to strong-arm you, but the guys in the offices with their heavy briefcases had protection from the government and the Old Bill. They were backed by a multitude of colleagues and companies with long histories. One would not know who to touch, who to kidnap and give a proper flogging as a warning to ease off. They were like the unseen hand of God, they could just reach out and take anything they wanted and there was not a damn thing that could be done about it.

The pub had historical significance and Vic knew that the longer he held on to it the more it would be worth. Records showed that the building had been originally built to be a drinking establishment. However, no one knew exactly when the place was constructed, but its interior gave some indication. Items in the basement and attic dated back to the 15th century. Vic sometimes wondered if the museums were only after the items tucked away untouched for centuries. He did not know what they were worth before Elizabeth told him about the lamp and the painting of the Prodigal Son, he only knew that they were old and very dusty. James Johnston and Sam McDougal, however, knew exactly how valuable they were. They always told him that the old dusty antiques could solve all of his financial problems only if he would find the time to dust them off and flog them, but he never believed them. Vic was never interested for he believed that he was keeping alive the memories of The Refuge and obviously the pub had held on to the historic memories of its previous owners. The antiques were a part of the spirit and soul of the establishment and they were not going anywhere.

McDougal and Johnston, the grifters that they were had different ideas. They would sneak out some of the smaller items and flogged them at yard sales and antique road shows. They would then spend the money at Vic's and would even give Vic himself a generous tip.......cheeky bastards!!!

Vic and Randy sketched a plan in their minds of how they were going to get the whisky from the basement, through the tunnel, to the docks and on to a waiting ship. The tracks in the tunnel would need some repairs as they were broken and badly damaged in some sections. They would have to get some lighting and they would most certainly have to get rid of those pesky rats.

Vic expected to be back in business providing that the sale of the whisky went as planned. He was going to transform the pub back to its former glory. He decided that he would begin the renovations from the bottom up. He has been thinking a lot about giving back the pub its old name, 'The Refuge'. He would return it to all its splendor and glory. He could not continue to operate with the name 'Vic's' because it was stained and tarnished with a negative stigma attached. Even with new décor and a touch of pomp, the name Vic's meant a safe house for the criminals and other degenerates of East London.

The discovery of the tunnel gave him inspiration and he couldn't contain his excitement. Randy read the expression on his face and even though he could not tell exactly what Vic was thinking he could sense the exuberance and he picked up the scent of untaxed and untraceable 'dosh'.

⋊ **33** ⋉

TRUTH AND RECONCILIATION

Vic *went over to see James* Johnston and found him slouched in a rocking chair in his den.

Vic said, 'What happened to you JJ? I haven't seen you for quite some time.'

JJ replied, 'I was kidnapped, blind folded and beaten up for no apparent reason. It was two of them. They held on to me for five days and told me it was for my own safety.'

'Do you know who kidnapped you?' asked Vic.

JJ replied, 'I don't know, one of the voices sounded very familiar, but I could not identify it.'

'When did they release you?' asked Vic.

JJ replied, 'They must have drugged me or something, but I woke up in this chair yesterday. I am still puzzled because I am yet to figure out why they kidnapped me then let me go just like that.'

Vic began to think and then he asked JJ, 'Do you by any chance know a bloke by the name of John Glass?'

'John Glass,' JJ said to himself searching his mind for answers. 'Now I remember the voice, it was him Johnny Glasgow, he kidnapped me.'

Vic repeated the name, 'Johnny Glasgow.' He thought

for a moment and then he recalled Kilbride referring to Glass as Johnny Glasgow.

JJ said, 'I haven't seen him in decades, I am surprised he didn't kill me. He looked at Vic with a forlorn expression on his face and he said, 'I am sorry son.'

'Sorry for what?' asked Vic.

'I should have told you years ago, but I feared for my life. The broken down James Johnston that you have gotten to know is as a direct result of Glasgow's actions. I refused to partake in his sinister schemes and I was banished from the circle. They made it seem as though I had gone crazy and as result I lost my science lab.'

'Tell me about this Johnny Glasgow,' Vic demanded.

'I knew all along that he was your father in law and I have known the truth behind the death of your wife and sons,' said JJ.

'What do you mean?' asked Vic.

'You were meant to be alone in the vehicle Vic,' said JJ looking away from Vic. 'Glasgow promised to give me back my lab if I sabotaged your car. You see Vic, I didn't know you back then and all I wanted to do was to continue practicing my medicine and to restore my honor.'

Vic now with clenched fists could not believe what he was hearing. He said, 'Are you telling me that my father in law gave you the contract to kill me?'

JJ replied, 'Yes, I am sorry. There is not a day that goes by that I don't think about it. I have always wanted to tell you, but I didn't know how well you would take it.'

Furiously Vic said, 'The only thing that is preventing me from choking you to death right now is because I need you!'

'I wouldn't blame you at all Vic,' said JJ. 'I longed to be put out of my misery. I thought the kidnappers would have done it, but all they did was to prolong my guilt.'

'Why did he want to kill me?' asked Vic.

'He never liked you,' replied JJ. 'He did not exactly approve of his only daughter marrying someone from the streets, but he bit his lips and accepted you out of love for her. He had chosen the perfect husband for her, but she didn't love him one bit. She loved you and she was willing to sacrifice her inheritance and cut him off if he didn't give the marriage his blessings'

'Continue,' said Vic.

'He was devastated when he heard that his daughter and grandsons had died in the accident and you got away unscathed. I haven't seen or heard from him since the day he called me on the telephone and threatened me. After that I went into hiding and started wearing disguises for he promised me death and he stressed that as sure as the sun shines he was going to kill me.'

'He must have kept you alive for a reason,' said Vic. 'Tell me, why did he change his name to Glass?'

'He didn't,' replied JJ. He just shortened it and eventually everybody thought that was his real name, but we knew the truth'

'Tell me about his past. I thought I knew the man, but recent events showed me how ignorant I am,' said Vic.

JJ positioned himself in his rocking chair and asked Vic to fetch him the half bottle of whisky sitting on the table in the living room. When Vic returned with the bottle he uncorked it and filled the glass JJ held in his hand.

'Have a seat son,' said JJ pointing to the chair beside the door.

Vic grabbed the chair and positioned it before JJ; he wanted to look in his eyes while he told the story behind John Glass, his murderous father in law.

'Have you heard the story of the Prodigal Son?' asked JJ.

''I have heard it recently. Why did you ask?' asked Vic.

'Because Johnny Glasgow's story is similar,' replied JJ. 'He came from a wealthy family and it is not too hard to figure that out for a city was named after them. His father saw that he was very greedy and he banished him. His father caught him trying to steal the formula for what would have become his greatest creation, the Scotsman whisky blend; he decided to banish John, because of his greed. Glasgow demanded his inheritance and his father gave him the money, after which he left Scotland and headed to London. He lost all is money in a few weeks and news got back to his father that he was living in squalor. Arthur Glasgow didn't want John to return home, so he contacted his old friend Patrick Carlisle the sea merchant. Patrick Carlisle agreed to take him under his wing and he became like a father to him. He paid for John to be enrolled in the navy to learn navigation and it would prove to be a worthwhile investment. He travelled the world with Carlisle trading and pilfering and got very wealthy from doing so and in the process he killed many men. After many years he decided to return home to show is father what he had achieved, but when he returned his father had died and everything was gone. The estate, the brewery, all their wealth had disappeared. He heard that his father may have been murdered for his secret formula and from then he vowed revenge on the people responsible for his family's lost fortune. He was at war for many decades with the other whisky producing families in Scotland as he searched for his father's missing formula and many lives were lost as a result. The violence and the killings became known as the 'Whisky Wars'.

'How did you two meet?' asked Vic

.JJ replied, 'I too along with McDougal, a bloke named One Eyed Jerry McCain and Robert 'Precision Bob' Nelson were also sailors and we eventually worked for Carlisle. As his trading routes expanded, he needed experienced sailors to haul his merchandise, so we quit the navy and got ourselves on his payroll.

Glasgow always acted like he was in charge when Carlisle was not around and we hated his guts. He would plan heists and force us to join in and if we didn't he would threaten us with blackmail. Most of the things you see in that basement at the pub were stolen by Glasgow. He was very reckless and I remember once he broke into the British Museum just for the fun of it. He stole a famous painting because he could relate to it. Carlisle was furious, but he couldn't return the painting, so he hid it in the basement and refused to allow Glasgow to sell it. Everything got out of hand when Patrick Carlisle passed away.'

He paused for a moment to wet his throat with some of the whisky he had in his glass and then he continued to tell his story.

He said, 'Jerry McCain and Robert Nelson disappeared under rather mysterious circumstances shortly after. As for McDougal and me, well you can see that we are barely getting by. I guess Glasgow didn't consider us a threat, but he stripped us of our possessions and literally threw us out into the streets. Many years passed before I saw him again and he invited me to join in his mysterious circle of influential men, but I refused and he destroyed my first science lab. I couldn't replace the lab that he had destroyed and the possibilities diminished further as I turned to heavy drinking to drown my failure as a man. He turned up out of nowhere one day and promised me a new lab if I sabotaged the brakes on your car. I was so desperate for a break that I took the job without thinking of the consequences, but I ensured that he built me the lab before I carried out the work and to my surprise he agreed to do it. I haven't seen him face to face since then, but I guess he is back now and I sense that he is out for blood.'

Vic grabbed a glass and poured himself some of JJ's whisky. He emptied the glass in seconds and then poured another.

'He has been using me all along, that bastard! I am going to get him before he gets me. I will continue to act the ignorant son-in-law until I get the opportunity to destroy him,' said Vic with blood stained eyes.

'Do you want my help with anything?' asked JJ as he emerged from his reminisce. 'Oh yes,' replied Vic. 'Come with me to the pub I have something to show you.'

JJ slowly got up from the chair and Vic noticed that he was limping. He said, 'They seem to have hurt you pretty badly.'

'Nah,' said JJ. 'I am a tough old geezer. My bones still ache from where they punched me up, but I will survive. Come on, let us go.'

On the way over to the pub, Vic told JJ about the whisky heist and his reunion with John Glass. He also told him about the Scotsman and how Glass killed Kenny Kilbride to recover it from the Kilbride distillery. JJ did not seem surprised to hear what he had done for he knew that Glass had been hunting the Scotsman for decades and the pursuit left a bloody trail from Britain all the way to the New World. Vic told him about the Mussolini brothers and their unfortunate demise caused by a poisoned bottle of Scotsman. JJ laughed at their folly, but Vic wasn't exactly amused for now they had to check every bottle. He was a criminal, but he had a conscience. He could not live with the thought of selling the whisky and not be sure that every bottle was safe to drink. JJ assured him that he would handle it.

When they arrived at the pub Randy and McDougal

were there waiting.

'Where have you been Vic?' asked McDougal. 'We were here wondering if you got bumped off or something.'

'As you can see I went to get JJ,' replied Vic. 'He is here to help with the whisky.'

'Nice to see you JJ,' said McDougal. 'It has been quite a while since we've caught up. How are you doing old friend?'

'I am still breathing,' replied JJ giving McDougal a friendly embrace.

'Come JJ, let me show you the whisky,' said Vic directing him to the door leading to the staircase.

'I see you have found the secret tunnel,' said JJ acknowledging the large hole in the wall.

Vic said 'Conveniently for us it leads straight to the docks, so we have a means of getting the whisky out without being seen. All we have to do now is find a bloke who owns a ship.'

'I know a guy, his name is Sanjay Gupta,' said JJ. 'He imports goods from all over the world from India to the Caribbean.'

'Can he be trusted?' asked Vic.

JJ said, 'No, he is a slimy bastard, but as long as you play straight with him, he won't rip you off. But if he smells a double cross he will sell you out to the highest bidder without even thinking twice about it.'

The men travelled down the tunnel to where the whisky was stashed.

'They are in this room,' said Vic pointing to the place.

JJ was surprised when he saw the barrels and bottles stacked high in boxes and crates in the room. He Said, 'There is enough whisky in here to water a country. How exactly did you pull this off Vic my boy?'

'It is a long story. My back was against the wall and I

was really concerned about my life, especially after the cockfight and the furor with the Mussolini brothers over the rigging. They threatened me, kidnapped my dog or so I thought. Right now I am not even sure if they did it and now I will never know.'

'Where did you put the bodies?' asked JJ.

'We sealed them in the room next door with a couple hundred rats. They are probably bones by now.'

'You will have to move them after a while. Get the bones as far away from you as possible. The coppers have some very sophisticated equipment these days to analyze forensic evidence. You may have to kill the rats for even they will be considered reliable witnesses when it comes to DNA evidence and all that stuff,' said JJ laughing.

Vic said, 'Yes, I definitely don't want to be ratted out.' Both men saw the humor and laughed hysterically.

'I don't know who to trust JJ.' said Vic. 'These past few days has taught me a great deal about human nature. The extent men would go to for revenge, the plotting and the scheming then cold blooded murder. That's just cold hearted and sinister.'

'Men have been doing that since the dawn of time,' said JJ.

Vic said, 'I am not saying that I am a saint for I would defend myself if my life was in danger. I would have hit Big Mike if someone hadn't gotten to him first.'

'Who is Big Mike?'

'Nobody,' replied Vic. 'Just some Irish bloke I had some problems with when I was at Pentonville. Either I have a guardian angel or I am being played like a puppet on a string. After witnessing what had happened to the Mussolini brothers, I am betting on both.'

'Who do you think is helping you to get rid of your enemies?' asked JJ.

'At first I thought it was the Mussolini brothers

protecting their investment, but now I know it had to have been Glass all along. He is both my guardian angel and my puppet master. I have to find a way to release myself from his grip, one of us must die.'

'Many men have tried what you are thinking and failed. Johnny Glasgow is a very smart man and I can assure you that getting him will not be easy,' said JJ

'I know,' said Vic. 'But I have to give it a try, this madman has to be stopped.'

'I agree,' said JJ. 'But you first have to figure out his plans and counteract them. You have to outsmart him if you want to beat him, so just continue following his orders while you set up your move.'

JJ started to look more closely at the whisky bottles. He identified all three distilleries just by looking at the crest which adorned the labels.

'I see you have paid a visit to Paisley, Dumbarton and Kilbride,' said JJ looking at Vic. 'You have got yourself a very valuable bounty here. These are the top three distilleries in Scotland. Did you know that?'

'I didn't know about them until a few nights ago,' said Vic looking at the bottles. 'It was John Glass who instructed us to rob these three. We were just planning on robbing the most isolated and least guarded brewery when Glass pounced upon us. Our plan was to go in rob it and get out of there as soon as possible, but all that changed when Glass turned up out of nowhere with his dogs and you can imagine how surprised I was to see him'

'Glass doesn't deal in surprises,' said JJ. 'He must have known that you would have turned up to his place even before you knew you would.'

'Do you think he would poison all the bottles in here?' asked Vic. 'I know I am paranoid, but I cannot see how he would have had the chance to do it. We left the lorries on the side of the road when we were doing the second heist, so that would be the only opportunity he could have had.'

'Which brewery did you rob first?' asked JJ.

'The Paisley place,' replied Vic.

'There you have it; we only need to test the whisky from there. Otherwise you could just call the man and ask him if he poisoned all the bottles,' said JJ amusingly. 'We will just test some of the bottles from each distillery if that makes you comfortable, but as cruel as Glasgow is I don't think he would do it. This is a very valuable lot you have here and he wants to make money and he is using you as his sales man.'

'He is going to be pissed when he discovers that his Tear Jerker went up in a ball of flame and I was not in it, but he probably knows that by now,' said Vic. 'He seems to have eyes and ears everywhere.'

Vic thought for a moment then he looked at JJ and said, 'Maybe you are right. McDougal would have had a thousand deaths by now with the amount of the whisky he has consumed. However, I don't trust John Glass, so I am still feeling a bit uneasy about it. He gave us one month to get rid of the loot and that's three weeks from now, so go ahead and test all the bottles we have time.'

JJ thought for a moment then said, 'It will take more than three weeks to test all those bottles. I will pretty much have to move my entire lab down here.'

'You don't need a lab to do the tests,' said Vic. 'I told you we have the rats for that.'

'Are you telling me that I will have to drip feed every single rat a sample of whisky?' asked JJ in a not so amused tone. 'Tell you what, don't even answer that, I have an idea. Why don't we mix all three brands together? This place is filled with oak barrels, so the liquid will be in its natural environment and we will only need one rat for the job.'

'I never thought about that,' said Vic. 'That's a brilliant idea and by doing that we will also disguise the blend and no one will be able to tell the brewery of origin. Brilliant! I will get Randy and McDougal to start preparing the oak barrels immediately we will start pouring first thing tomorrow. There is a lot of work to do and just thinking about it makes my head hurt. We could really do with some more hands, and we could have had enough manpower if it wasn't for those three bastards Harry, Fred and Tony British.'

JJ said, 'Let us go see Sanjay Gupta tomorrow and try to convince him to buy the whole shipment.'

'No,' said Vic. 'Let us wait until we have rebottled and relabeled the whisky before we go out and seek a buyer. I don't want to let anyone in until I know that the coppers are not on our trail. We have to keep our eyes and ears open.'

The men left the basement and went back up the stairs to the pub. They found Randy and McDougal playing darts. Vic told them the plan and they were impressed.

'When are we going to have a taste of the new blend?' asked McDougal with dried throat as he aimed and miss the bull's eye that was needed to win the game.

'You owe me ten quid,' said Randy laughing.

'Vic distracted me,' retorted McDougal

'No, the thought of whisky distracted you,' said Vic. 'There is a lot of work to do and you are up here arguing about ten quid. We have the tracks to repair, the oak barrels to prepare, the bottles to be emptied, stripped, washed, relabeled and then refilled, so we need to get a move on it now or maybe you are Flash Gordon and you can do all that in the blink of an eye.'

'Where should we start?' asked a subdued Randy.

'You and McDougal go check out the barrels and choose the ones in the best condition. God knows how long they have been down there, so make sure you check for critters.'

'What are you going to do?' asked Randy. 'I noticed that since we came out of Pentonville you have been ordering me around. Remember I saved your ass Vic, so I deserve some respect from you.'

'I don't have time to squabble with you Randy, I have somewhere to be,' said Vic as he walked towards the exit of the pub. 'Come on JJ let me give you a ride back to your place.'

✂ 34 ✂

THE LAST APPOINTMENT

Vic *always dreaded visiting this place.* This was where *both* his angels and demons lay awaiting him to breathe his last breath before being thrown into a deep eternal slumber. The outside world was purgatory, but when he was through the gates of the final resting place he felt at home and it scared him for he was not ready. He had things to do and he needed truth and reconciliation to set his mind at ease. As he approached the large gates he could feel the piercing eyes of the gargoyles sitting in their usual place on the huge columns. He wondered if they were there to drag the cursed souls to the depths of hell and prevent the unworthy from entering the place of the privileged dead.

The cemetery looked like a city with skyscrapers making a skyline. The grass was well manicured and the environment was green and lush. Vic could hear the birds chirping in the large trees which dominated the cemetery. He walked along the paved walkway leading to the place where his family rested. He observed the large mausoleums and the huge tombstones that gave the appearance of a city street. The water lilies sat beautifully on top of the water in a small pond while fishes of various sizes and colors navigated their small domain. He stopped to look at them and thought of the wonderful adornment they would make on a platter filled with roasted potatoes and vegetables.

As he approached his destination he noticed that some of the graves had fresh flowers lying on top indicating the existence of living caring relatives. He noticed that other graves had withered flowers and others had no flowers at all and he wondered if those people had no living relatives who cared enough to place flowers on their graves. Generations that have vanished from the face of the earth had long sufferers still trying to come to terms with their death with expressions of regular visits and the laying of flowers. Some of the graves were centuries old and he thought about those people and the fact that their bloodline may still exist today not knowing that they have relatives dwelling in the city of the dead. He became sad and was deeply hurt by the thought that families can be lost and forgotten over time and the grave in which their bone lay was the only indication that they ever existed. He thought about what would happen to him when he died for he had no family and the people whom he thought were his friends were nothing but opportunists looking for their next score.

Vic hadn't visited the place in months, the longest since his release from Bedlam. The guilt was still with him and he could not look at the stones which bear the names of his wife and sons. He thoughtfully placed the flowers he had purchased from the flower shop, near the entrance of the cemetery, on top of the graves. He choked as the tears came pouring down his cheek and he screamed out as though a spear had pierced his heart.

He looked intently at the three headstones which underneath marked and indicated the remains of his family. He then looked around at the expensive mausoleums scattered all over the cemetery and it saddened him that he could not afford to house his beloved family in a more prestigious resting place.

He wept as he remembered the days of sobriety when he moved with purpose and dignity. Kilbride's last words kept haunting him. He knew that he wasn't intoxicated at a level whereby he could not control a car. He had driven home even more inebriated and made it in one piece. '*Did Glass really have something to do with the accident? Well of course he did. JJ had already said that much.*'

He sat down with his back pressed against the headstone of his wife. He was tired and he longed for solitude and eternal rest. He knew he was living dangerously and it would only be a matter of time before his chickens came home to roost and Little John and Lucky and a multitude of enemies were sure to be there to partake in the lynching of Vic '*The Slick*' Montgomery.

Vic not realizing he was speaking out loud said, 'They do not really know me, my inner feelings, my pain, my sorrows. I am broken and I long to be healed.'

'Repent of your sins my son and you shall surely be healed and you will come to rest in this place a clean and pure man,' said a voice behind him.

Vic was startled and he jumped up and assumed a defensive position.

'There is still time Vic and I am sure that you will be victorious. Your enemies will be made known and if you play your cards right, you will make it out alive or maybe you would prefer to settle here sooner rather than later,' said the voice.

'Who are you?' shouted Vic looking towards a huge tomb a few meters from where he was standing. The old man stepped out from behind the tomb.

He smiled and said, 'Victor, I am your father.'

Vic looked squarely in his eyes and said, 'My father is unknown to me. That bastard never cared; he left before I opened my eyes. You seem like a nice old fella, but I am not in the mood for trickery, I have enough of that to deal with in my day job.'

The old man kept the gaze that Vic started and he was holding on firm. Vic noticed that the old man's eyes were genuine. He looked weathered, but there was still something intriguing about him.

'Who are you?' asked Vic sternly.

He responded, 'My name is Robert Nelson, but my old friends call me Precision Bob. I am the caretaker here.'

Vic examined him closely. He recalled that JJ had mentioned a Precision Bob in one of his stories about something to do with a darts tournament and him being the best player to ever throw a dart in The Refuge. He had also mentioned that Robert Nelson was presumed dead and that he used to work for Patrick Carlisle.

Vic pretended that he never heard the name before and he gave him a blank stare.

'After your mother died, I couldn't take care of you myself, so I left you at the orphanage in the care of the nuns. I used to check in on you regularly, but then I had to leave the country in a hurry. John Glasgow had begun to clean house after Patrick Carlisle died and he was on the hunt to punish dissention.'

He looked at Vic with venom in his eyes and said, 'I never liked that bastard Glasgow and he knew that, so naturally I would become his first target and like a coward I fled. I now know that I should have had more courage to stand up to him, but I did it to protect you. You were my only remaining blood tie and I could not bear the thought of you getting hurt.'

Vic looked at the man that stood before him. He wanted to reach out and hug him, but his pride prevented him for doing so. He wanted to believe the old man, but his mind was too confused to make a clear judgment on what he was hearing.

Robert Nelson broke Vic's thoughts and said, 'I spent many years in the Caribbean where I made a living as a fisherman. I got myself a boat and for the first time I felt free in the embrace of the sea and the sun.

'That explains his tanned and sandy look. His face is weary and he looked tired. This poor broken soul standing before me, could he really be my father? Should I hug him or let him stand there and suffer the wrath of my rejection?'

Vic looked at him and said, 'Since you are my father, how come we don't share the same last name?'

'I registered you under your mother's surname at the orphanage, so that they couldn't trace you. If you check with the birth registration office you will find that you were born Victor George Nelson. We can go there tomorrow if you want proof,' said Nelson.

Vic now wondered if Glass knew about this and was one step ahead as usual.

'How can I be sure that Glass didn't put you up to this? When did you come back to England?' asked Vic abrasively.

'I came back in time for your wedding. I was there in disguise, JJ fixed me up real good,' replied Nelson.

'Does JJ know about me, does he know that I am your son?' Vic asked.

'Yes, he is the only person who knows. He was the only person I trusted back then and he kept his mouth shut.'

Vic thought for a moment and he surmised that it was a strong possibility that JJ may have revealed the information under duress.

'I am assuming that you have been watching me and

you know everything, so I will skip the preamble. I am not into this daddy stuff, so we will never speak of this again,' said Vic.

'John Glass must die. We have to get rid of him otherwise we will never find peace,' said Nelson looking at the headstones. 'I never had a chance to hold my grandsons or to buy them presents at Christmas and bring them to the ice cream shop on their birthdays.'

Tears ran down his face as he placed the flowers he held in his hands on the graves.

He said, 'All because of Glass I lost my family and he took yours away from you as well. We must work together to rid ourselves of this evil pestilence. Just tell me what you want me to do and it is done.'

Vic laid his hand gently on the old man's shoulder and said, 'Come with me back to the pub. We could surely use a couple more hands to get the whisky bottled up and ready for market.'

The sun was starting to set on the cemetery as the men made their way to the exit. Vic thought about what he had heard and he was filled with both anger and glee. The man walking beside him moved exactly as he did. He was like his shadow walking in sync with his form. Vic started to notice a slight resemblance as they both had the same strong bony face and slim stature. He let go of all the pride that kept him from embracing the stranger and he wished that he would get the opportunity to hear his stories. Stories of long voyages and adventure that will make him proud to call the old man his father. He wanted a legacy the same that Glass coveted. He still had time to build a family and make a fresh start not committing the same mistakes he made which caused him to lose everything. He thought about Elizabeth and how she would make a lovely wife and mother. Perhaps the old man would get the opportunity to hold his grandkids. He smiled as he remembered the passion he felt whenever he had sex with her. She helped him to rediscover love, but he held back a piece of his heart for he didn't trust her completely. Either she was a very good detective or she was being fed information. She knows more than she let off and he knew that he will have to be mindful of her.

Vic emancipated himself from the harness of his mind and looked over at Nelson and said, 'We will pick up JJ on the way. I want us to start bottling tonight; we have to get rid of the whisky a week from now. Glass gave us one month to do it, but I want us to do it in two weeks, so that we can prepare for an attack on him.'

'I agree,' said Nelson. 'If I know that conniving bastard I bet he will want to collect early, so we must have a clear view of the playing field.

⊰ 35 ⊱

THE MASTER BLEND

The three men arrived at the pub as the last glimmer of the sun evaded East London. They entered the pub and found Randy sitting by the bar with a silver mug to his mouth chugging down the last mouthful of beer.

He looked at Vic and said, 'You sure took your time. We are done with the barrels they were all in good condition, so it didn't take us long.'

Vic handed him the large parcel of fish and chips that he had bought in Hackney Downs.

'Hey McDougal,' shouted Randy. 'Our master brought us some good old British fish and chips.'

'I love fish, but I can't stand the grease,' shouted back McDougal. 'Mark my words, soon enough the fish and chips that you all love will give half this country coronary disease. You thought world war two was bad; compare that to thirty years from now and the amount dying from heart disease. Pour me a mug of that brew; at least I can piss it out.'

The men heard the toilet flushed and McDougal emerged drying his wet hands on his shirt. He was startled to see the new addition to the gang. He wiped his eyes with his now dry hands and peered closely at the man standing beside Vic and JJ. He went over to him and shook his hand and said, 'I can't believe it! Precision Bob, is it really you?'

'If it is not me, then who else could it be?' responded Precision Bob with mock sarcasm. 'Hello old friend, it has been decades since I have seen you. I am happy to know that the three of us are still alive.'

'I am happy to see that I am not the only old broken down geezer around here. Come lets go catch up over a game of darts,' said McDougal directing Nelson to the dart board.

'Who is that old bloke?' inquired Randy.

'That is Vic's old man,' responded JJ.

'Is this true Vic?' asked Randy.

'I am starting to believe it,' replied Vic.

He immediately changed the subject and said, 'How many barrels do we have Randy?'

'We have about one hundred plus the ones already with whisky in them,' replied Randy.

'We are going to empty and mix all the whisky together. I need to be certain that it is not contaminated,' said Vic.

'We don't have a container big enough to hold all the whisky, so how exactly are we going to mix everything together?' asked Randy.

'We will measure it out and ensure that we use the same consistency in all the barrels. It is not rocket science, just basic mixology,' responded JJ.

'Ok gentlemen,' said Vic. 'Let us go to the basement and get started we will be working through the night.'

Vic checked the front door of the pub to make sure that it was locked. He then led the way to the basement and the men followed in single file.

Robert Nelson was surprised when he saw the volume of whisky stored in the basement. He looked a Vic and gave him a respectful nod as was to say, well done son, you made your old man proud. Randy rolled out the first empty barrel and then went back for two barrels filled with whisky from the Paisley and Dumbarton distilleries and JJ grabbed a bottle from Kilbride's place along with his measuring and testing apparatus.

He said, 'We are going to test a small sample of all three blends together. We will give a drop to a rat and see how he reacts to it. If he is not belly up after a couple minutes then I would say it has not been contaminated.'

The men watched intently as JJ handled his equipment like a true professional. He didn't need his white coat, but he adorned himself in it to give him the appearance as though he was in his lab cooking up his usual concoctions.

'Fetch me a rat,' he instructed Randy.

Randy went over to the small birdcage which they had found earlier and decided that it would be a good place to put the test subjects. He came back holding the rat by its tail with his hand stretched away from his body. JJ poured some of the whisky in a glass container and instructed Randy to hold the rat's face over it. The rat hesitated for a bit as he sniffed the strange looking liquid before him. He stuck out his small tongue and collected some. He spun his body around as the alcohol made contact with his taste glands. He then reached in for a second taste and this time he was in no hurry. He did not react as the first and the men realized that the rat was enjoying the new blend.

Vic noticed that McDougal was anxious to indulge, but he told him to be patient and wait to see what will happen to the rat. After a few minutes McDougal was satisfied with the health of the rat and he snatched up the bottle with the rest of the mixture and tasted it slowly. His reaction was quite similar to the rats' as he shook his head from side to side. He let out a sound as if he was releasing steam and then took a large gulp.

He turned to Nelson and said, 'I think you should try this Bob. It has a familiar taste, but I can't figure out where I have tasted it before.'

Nelson took the bottle from McDougal and poured some in a glass and carefully inspected the golden liquid inside. He said, 'It sure does have a distinct color and a familiar scent. My nostrils have not been blessed with this scent for a very long time. It smells like the essence of the Scottish highlands.'

He then said the name that sent chills down Vic's spine.

He said, 'Arthur Glasgow! This is Arthur Glasgow's formula. I can tell by the scent. He never did get the chance to perfect his formula for the Scotsman. He created many wonderful blends, but his life work was to make the perfect tasting whisky that embodies the very soul and essence of Scotland.'

'I have been to Arthur Glasgow's place,' said JJ. 'Let me have a smell.' He held the glass to his nostrils and inhaled deeply. 'Ah, yes,' he said. 'I can remember visiting Arthur at his home in Scotland and his lab was dominated with this scent. He must have tricked his treacherous neighbors by splitting the formula into three parts. Each of the three distilleries has been brewing one part of the formula.'

'Are you saying that the bottles Glass took from Kilbride's place was not the Scotsman?' asked Vic.

'I doubt it,' said Nelson. 'Glasgow did not reach the production stage, but he had the bottles ready and waiting, so John Glasgow must have filled those up and somehow planted it at Kilbride's place.'

'I think you are right about that,' said Vic.

Nelson said, 'Arthur Glasgow's lab was very secure, so

I doubt that the formula was stolen from underneath his nose. That leads me to two theories. The first is that the prodigal son Johnny Glasgow stole the formula from his father's lab and sold it to the competing brewers. The second is that Arthur Glasgow intentionally allowed the three breweries to acquire his formula in an effort to conceal his master blend.'

'I am going with the first theory,' said Vic. 'That crafty bastard John Glass. He knew who stole his father's formula, but he needed the man power to get it back. This is very confusing!'

'I see what you mean,' said McDougal. 'He planned it down to every last detail. He had everything covered except the muscles and our services were not too hard to acquire.'

'Kilbride seemed to have known the truth and John Glasgow killed him before he got a chance to tell us,' said McDougal looking at Nelson.

'Kilbride was a good man. No one caused as much damage to the Glasgow family as Johnny Glasgow. He laid ruin to his family's entire estate,' said Nelson. 'You didn't kill your family son, Johnny Glasgow did.'

'He knows. I have already told him about that,' said JJ in a sorrowful tone.

Vic with venom in his voice said, 'All those years that I have been languishing behind bars and in that lunatic asylum with the guilt and remorse of me murdering my lovely wife and my beautiful kids. I almost lost my god damn mind, while that bastard plotted and waited to use me to do his dirty deeds.' He looked at the men and said, 'Thank you for being here, especially you Randy. You have stuck with me through it all and I appreciate that. JJ and McDougal you too have helped to sustain me and I learned a lot from your stories. And you old man who purport to be my father, and if it is indeed so, I feel blessed to have met you and tonight I can confidently say that it is the first in a very long time that I have felt that I am among family.'

'Let us have a toast,' announced McDougal eager for another taste of the Scotsman. Each man grabbed a glass and filled it with the blended brew.

They held up their glasses and McDougal said, 'To family and friendship, the world will be a better place when the two become one.'

'Aye,' shouted the men in unison.

'And may we eradicate from the face of the earth that demon John Glass,' said Randy.

'Aye,' shouted the men again in unison.

'Now let us get to work,' instructed Vic. 'We have to start working on the tunnel tomorrow and I have to go and see that bloke down at the docks. What's his name again JJ?'

'Gupta,' replied JJ.

Nelson's ears perked up when he heard the name.

He said, 'Are you talking about Sanjay Gupta, the exporter?'

'Yes. Why?' responded JJ.

'You know he used to work for Glasgow right?' he said looking at Vic.

'I don't know about that,' responded JJ. 'What I do know is that he was Patrick Carlisle's man in India and that he bought up the dockyard and the ships from the Carlisle estate. But I wouldn't be surprised though because Glasgow seems to have his hands in everything.'

'I will go with you to see him tomorrow Vic,' said Nelson.

'No,' said Vic. 'It is best if you stay away from anybody that would recognize you. I want him to think I am naïve and if he is working for Glass then maybe we can convince him to work for us. I learned from JJ that he has a very strong allegiance to money.'

'You are right about that,' said Nelson. 'You go feel him out and if he doesn't look you squarely in the eyes then he cannot be trusted.'

'This bloke is really your father Vic. I am happy to see someone else dish out some instructions for a change,' said Randy followed by his annoying laughter.

The five men toiled through the night until six a.m. and they had successfully blended the whisky from the three distilleries. Some were rebottled and the rest remained in their oak abode. Vic was pleased with the work they had done and he congratulated his colleagues. They departed the basement and agreed to meet back there at four pm when they would start working on the tunnel and if all goes well with the Gupta meeting they would be transferring the whisky to the docks that same night. Vic requested that Nelson stay at the pub and told him that he will serve as watchman for the remainder of the operation. His job was to look out for suspicious vehicles and blokes in the vicinity of the pub. Nelson was pleased with his job description and he promised that he will keep a sharp eye out for danger just like in the days when he used to sail the high seas.

⚼ 36 ⚼

THE EXPORTER

Sanjay *Gupta's office was cluttered* with maps of various sizes. The walls were covered with an assortment of stuffed sea creatures. There was a large aquarium filled with various types of fish swimming around contentedly in their small world. Above the huge oak desk hung a sign with the word 'Refuge' written on it and Vic quickly figured that this must have been Patrick Carlisle's office originally. The back of the big antique looking leather chair was facing them. It spun around quickly as if it was lying on a ball bearing. The small frail figure sitting in it said, 'Welcome gentlemen, and please sit down. I have been expecting you.'

Vic shot JJ a quick look and JJ looked at Gupta and said, 'Thank you for agreeing to see us at short notice, but we have a business proposition for you.'

'I have known you for a very long time James Johnston and after you called I cleared all my appointments,' said Gupta in a slightly sounding sarcastic tone.

'You are always a sarcastic bastard,' said JJ in a friendlier manner.

'Pardon my ill manners gentlemen. Would you like a

drink? Some brandy, perhaps?'

'That's why we are here,' said Vic cutting through the chase. 'You are an exporter and we want you to do some exporting for us.'

'What is wrong with this young fella James? Have you not thought him the art of doing business with a tradesman?' said Gupta.

'I haven't had the chance to get around to that,' said JJ jokingly.

Gupta laughed out hysterically and then all of a sudden he looked Vic squarely in the eyes with a now serious look on his face.

He said, 'You must buy something from me first. If I sell you bullshit you must buy it. No real tradesman will buy from a person unless that person first buys from him. I offer you some brandy and you didn't even have the courtesy to respectfully refuse my hospitality. Instead you cut me off and went straight into business. I am a busy man and if you don't know the basics of doing business then you should get the hell out of my god damn office!'

'He is young and has much to learn,' interjected JJ saving Vic from the lashing of Gupta's tongue.

'My apologies, I will have that drink you offered now, thank you,' said Vic politely.

Gupta poured three glasses and laid them on the desk. He raised his glass and the men followed suit. 'To health, wealth and long life,' he said before pouring the contents of the glass down his throat. 'Now what can I do for you young man.'

Vic did not know where to start and it took him a minute to collect his thoughts. Gupta had thrown him off guard with his small stature and over powering personality. He could see why Gupta made it in business. He was unassuming, but as sharp as a razor.

He finally said, 'We have a large quantity of whisky

that we want to get as far away as possible from this island, but we want payment up front. Do you know anybody overseas who would be willing to buy it all?'

'Well, it depends,' replied Gupta.

'Depends on what?' asked Vic.

Gupta replied, 'It bloody well depends on if you are selling a high quality tasting whisky or some diluted down piss! I will of course need to sample the merchandise before I can quote you a price that I think my buyers would be willing to pay.'

'Give him the bottle JJ,' instructed Vic.

Gupta inspected the bottle and said, 'Hmmm, no label I see, but it does have a nice color. I hope it bloody well taste as good as it looks.'

He grabbed a clean glass and unscrewed the cover of the bottle. He poured out a shot and slowly brought the glass to his nose. He took some quick whiffs like a master connoisseur, but his face remained expressionless.

He said, 'It smells good.' He twirled the liquid in the glass and observed the motion as though he was a chemistry student conducting an experiment. 'It has body. Where did you say you got this from?'

'I didn't say,' replied Vic in a sharp tone. 'Are you planning on tasting it or are you just going to sit there and play with it.'

Gupta held the glass to his mouth and the whisky barely made contact with his lips. He said, 'A very interesting blend, but not to my taste. I am a brandy guy, but I am sure I can get someone to buy the whole lot. How soon can you get it on the docks?'

'Just give us a price and a down payment on behalf of your client and you will have it here before daybreak,' said Vic.

'My apologies young man, I seem to have underestimated your prowess, but I now see that you are a very shrewd business man. How much of it do you have?' he asked.

'We have five thousand bottles and each bottle can easily be turned into two and still maintain its taste and consistency,' replied Vic.

Gupta scratched his beard and said, 'I will convince my client to pay £10 per bottle, so that's £50, 000 and that's a healthy sum if I might had.'

'You complimented me a few minutes ago and now you are trying to take me for a fool,' said Vic. 'Come JJ, let us go, I thought this bloke was a serious tradesman, but he is nothing but a side winder.'

'Ok, £15 per bottle and that's the final offer. If you don't like it go take your business elsewhere,' said Gupta with a raised voice.

'Let me repeat what I said earlier,' said Vic. 'Each bottle can be transformed into two and it can even stretch further if you are selling it to someone who doesn't know the difference between whisky and rubbing alcohol, so you and your clients are poised to make a lot of money. I will not accept anything less than £20 per bottle.'

'You must be out of your bloody mind!' shouted Gupta. 'Twenty quid! You must be having a laugh mate. James I think your friend here needs to go see a psychiatrist.'

'He spent many years with them,' said JJ. 'So, I think you should consider the offer and if I know him well enough I can say that he has already decided to sell the whisky to you. It is now up to you to accept the price.'

'And what if I don't accept it?' said Gupta bravely.

'Then I cannot be held responsible for what will happen to you next.'

'Ok, ok, accepted,' said Gupta in a weary tone. 'But, no bloody way I am giving you £50, 000 now. I am only giving you £20, 000 and another twenty with every delivery of one thousand two hundred and fifty bottles. Excuse me for one minute gentlemen I am going to call my client and if he agrees to buy the whisky I will pay you the money on his behalf.'

Gupta got up from his desk and disappeared in a room to the back of the office. JJ looked at Vic and whispered, 'Why didn't you mention the whisky in the barrels?'

'I will explain it to you when we get out of here,' responded Vic.

Gupta returned to the room after several minutes and handed Vic an envelope filled with twenty pound notes in bands of a thousand. Vic pulled out a couple random £1000 stacks and examined the notes carefully. He was satisfied that they were real. Gupta walked over to the window of his office overlooking the harbor. Vic got up out of his chair and went over to where Gupta was standing and followed his line of vision, which ended up on a black ship with the name Saint Sebastian written in bold white letters on the side and underneath that was written the words Voyager of the Caribbean in smaller letters. Gupta looked up at Vic and said, 'My client wants everything here by tomorrow evening. Can you deliver?'

'I will deliver,' replied Vic.

'Ok, I will meet you here tomorrow evening.'

'Make sure you have the rest of the money,' said Vic.

'It will be here,' Gupta assured him.

The men bid each other farewell and the meeting ended. Gupta sat back in his chair and looked at the bottle sitting on top of his desk. He picked it up and poured some in his glass. He drank this time without hesitation and savored the taste of the elusive Scotsman in his mouth. He was disturbed by a heavy knock on the door. 'It is open,' he shouted in an annoyed tone. The door opened and a man walked in followed by another. 'Oh, it is you,' said Gupta. 'How on earth did you get here so quickly? I only just spoke to you on the phone.'

'I am always around,' replied John Glass. 'You did a good job with Vic; I suppose he didn't suspect anything?'

'I did exactly as you commanded, he suspects nothing' replied Gupta.

'I know you did, I have been watching,' said Glass. 'I have cameras installed all over this place.' He walked over to the desk and held the whisky bottle up to his face and said, 'Have they successfully blended the whisky?'

'Yes they did,' replied Gupta.

'Does it taste exactly like the bottle I gave you?'

'Yes, it does. I couldn't tell the difference,' replied Gupta.

'Just as I had anticipated,' said Glass laughing.

The second man laughed as well and he stared ominously at Gupta.

'Well, I think your job here is done,' said Glass.

'What do you mean?' asked Gupta.

'The old man always liked you and I must admit you are very good at what you do,' said the second man walking slowly towards his stationary victim.

'You wouldn't dare!' shouted Gupta.

The man slowly screwed the silencer to his pistol and said, 'It has to be this way Sanjay. Please forgive me.'

Gupta screamed out as though he had already been shot, but his scream was silenced by the silent bullet that pierced his heart.

'Put him in one of the large barrels on the ship. We will drop him and Dawson off at sea tomorrow night,' instructed Glass.

On the way back to the pub JJ asked his question again. 'Now tell me what exactly is going on Vic. Why didn't you tell Gupta about the rest of the whisky?'

Vic replied, 'Nelson is right. Gupta is working for Glass. Did you notice the security camera?'

'Yes, I saw the big white contraption hanging off the wall,' responded JJ.

'No, not that one,' said Vic. 'There was a small camera in the ceiling next to the light bulb.'

'Oh! I didn't see that one. You are one smart son of a snake Vic Montgomery,' said JJ laughing.

'I think they are planning on sailing tomorrow on that black ship in the harbor and I know where they are going,' said Vic.

'John Glass strikes again,' said JJ.

Vic said, 'I think they are planning on killing us all and burying us at sea. Poor old Gupta is already dead and he doesn't even know it.'

'Yeah, I liked that old geezer,' said JJ mournfully.

⚔ **37** ⚔

THE DOCKS

The two men arrived back at the pub and found Nelson, McDougal and Randy hard at work in the tunnel. They had managed to repair the broken tracks and were just about to test the trolleys.

Vic said, 'Well done men you have done a fine job repairing these broken tracks.'

Randy looked happy to see him and he asked, 'How did it go with the exporter Vic?'

'Vic replied, 'It went well. We are twenty thousand pounds richer and we found a buyer for all the bottled whisky and he thinks we are making the delivery tomorrow night.'

'What about the whisky in the barrels?' McDougal asked.

'I am saving those for when I renovate the pub. I promised myself that I will restore it to its former splendor and glory,' replied Vic.

'I would love to see this placed fixed up,' reminisced Nelson. 'I can remember exactly how it used to be. The lights gleaming from the huge chandeliers illuminated the beautiful wall paper. The comfortable seats and soft carpet that adorned the floors gave the place a look of elegance.'

'Patrick Carlisle sure knew how to run a pub, no offence to you Vic,' said McDougal.

'None taken,' said Vic dryly. 'Come let us get a move on. We must get the bottles on to the Saint Sebastian before day break.'

'What about tomorrow night?' Randy asked.

Vic replied, 'We will turn up tomorrow night to complete the deal as agreed.'

'You sure know how to cut it close,' said Randy.

'I have learned that to win you must always have the element of surprise on your side,' said Vic. 'Furthermore, our adversary is very smart, so we have to be twice as smart to defeat him.'

The men worked throughout the night and managed to conceal the whisky bottles on the ship without being spotted. Things were going according to plan and it would all be over soon.

'McDougal get your biggest Lorry ready for tonight. I am going in with Randy to do the deal and I want the three of you to make your way to the ship while we haggle with Gupta and his client. I want you to be ready to sail away if things go downhill. I assume that the passage has already been booked with the Port Authority, so the paper work should be in order.'

The men met in the pub for a final walk through of the end game strategy. The lorry was ready and the three old men made their way to the tunnel. Vic and Randy double checked their pistols as they sat in the lorry. 'This is it,' said Vic looking at Randy.

'Let's do it,' said Randy bravely.

The men pulled up before Gupta's dockyard and surveyed the premises to see if there was any suspicious activity taking place. Satisfied that it was safe, the men proceeded to drive through the gates. They could make out the silhouette of a person standing in the dockyard waiting for them to park and alight from the vehicle.

Vic pulled up and instructed Randy to be ready. They both exited the vehicle and walked towards the silhouette. The shadowy shape assumed form and Vic and Randy almost fainted when they saw Peter Carlisle standing before them.

'I thought you were dead,' said Randy.

'I thought so too,' said Peter Carlisle.

'I assume that you too work for John Glass,' said Vic.

'I work for no one!' shouted Peter Carlisle. 'Disarm yourselves gentlemen,' he said pointing a rifle at them.

Vic and Randy relieved themselves of their pistols and they now felt light and vulnerable.

Peter Carlisle looked away from them to observe the buildings that lined the dockyards and said, 'My Grandfather owned this dockyard and he placed it in a trust for me. I only found out about it when they took me to the hospital after you left me for dead. They must have run my name through the database and found out that I was from a wealthy family. I tricked them into thinking I had amnesia, so they told me everything I needed to know about my Grandfather's wealth and legacy.'

Vic and Randy still could not get over the surprise of seeing Peter Carlisle alive and well. The worse part about it was that he had them in a subdued position and the game was in his favor.

Peter said, 'See, you did me a favor Vic, thanks to you and your mate Randy standing there, I am now a very, very wealthy man, and you are still just a small-timer Vic, you don't think big enough, you are a loser and will always be a loser.

'He paused to catch his breath and to savor the moment of his superior position over the two men that he had waited for patiently for many years. He continued to speak again, 'I have always been one step ahead of you. I knew about your little Scotland trip….. I knew about Big Mike. In fact I orchestrated the hotel hit. The Mussolini brothers did the job at the hotel because they thought they were going to get you. I did not want anyone to spoil the plans I had for you, so I set them up and took them out of the way,' he said in a sinister tone.

Vic and Randy stood frozen in front of the rifle and the man holding it. The man had a look of satisfaction plastered all over his face and he seemed ready to shoot.

He said, 'I planted enough evidence that could be used to put you away for a lifetime, and you would have been hanged if the death penalty was still in effect. There are many players in this game Vic and if you were smart enough you would have read the play a long time ago.'

'We made a mistake,' pleaded Randy. 'We never meant to hurt you so badly.'

'Oh, but you did. I am lucky to be alive after the trashing you gave me,' said Peter.

He turned his attention to Vic and said, 'I hope you enjoyed Elizabeth. I hope you don't think it was anything serious. She was just out to pleasure herself. She is always on the search for her next pleasure trip and she likes to play with the bad boys. She played you all along and she was using you Vic. She never wanted you, and was only fishing for information.'

'You are a total psychopath Peter, you really need help. I know some people who can help you at my request,' said Vic

Peter didn't seem to hear a word that came out of Vic's mouth, but continued with his diatribe.

He said, 'I have been watching you since the day I left that wretched hospital. I know how you think, and oh, I almost forgot about Francis, lovely dog, he loved me so much, but the barking and the drooling started to get on my nerves, so I had to put him to sleep. Did you like the little note? I bet the ear gave you a big scare.'

Vic was now fuming and he wished he could reach out and choke Peter Carlisle to death, but the rifle had him pinned down and he felt like his feet were buried in concrete. Peter noticed Vic's rage and said, 'You are like my little puppet. So emotional Vic, the slightest thing get your feathers ruffled up and your actions become predictable. Anyway, I want to introduce you to someone. I think you know him very well, or do you?'

'Hello Victor,' John Glass made his presence known as he emerged from the darkness with a pistol in his hand. 'I see you managed to negotiate a deal within two weeks, well done. By the way Gupta won't be joining us tonight for you see I am his client as a matter of fact, Peter and I were his only clients. He knew too much so we had to take out a permanent gag order if you know what I mean.

Vic looked at him and said, 'I am not surprised to see you here John, but I must say that seeing Peter is what surprises me the most.

John Glass said, 'Now that we have the surprises out of the way I can tell you exactly how I feel about you. You are scum Vic. Always have been and always will be. You consider yourself to be a genius and a great strategist thinking you could outsmart me. The only loyal person you had around you was Randy, may his soul rest in peace.'

He wasted no time. He got Randy between the eyes with the German Luger. It was so sudden, even Peter Carlisle was a bit shocked. He then pointed the gun at Vic and continued with the eulogy.

'We bought everyone around you, even your enemies. We did not approach the Jamaicans because we knew that they are loyal to no one. They would have probably taken my money and vanished with it like what Tony

British did with your lorry. We knew all the details of your plans. You think you could kill my daughter and grandchildren and get away Scots free? Now, you will pay with your life. You were smart to have switched vehicles with Harry or else you would have been dead. I hope you didn't think that McDougal made the shot, the tanker was rigged with explosives and I was tracking it on GPS and I patiently watched my monitors while the clock ticked away.'

'You killed your own daughter, you murdering bastard!' shouted Vic.

The gun was still locked on Vic and Glass ordered him to get down on his knees. Obeying he fell to the ground and closed his eyes. He was ready. He had let go of all the problems in his life and had no tricks left. Randy was gone, Francis was gone, and Elizabeth was a snake. He was ready to meet his maker.

'It was unfortunate what happened to my beautiful daughter and grandsons, but I have learned to live with it Vic!' Shouted Glass. 'You could have been standing here beside me and Peter, but you drowned yourself in self-pity and did not earn your place among wealthy and influential men.'

Vic heard a shot rang out and he slowly open his eyes to see who got hit once he did not feel the pain of a bullet burning his flesh and piercing through his inner organs. He saw Glass standing frozen like a statue with the gun still pointed at him. He checked himself again for impact and found no wound. He heard another shot and he saw when Peter Carlisle fell. He looked back at Glass who was now on his knees. The place fell completely silent and Vic scanned the place looking for the shooter.

After a few minutes Tony British appeared from the darkness and said in a nonchalant tone, 'Vic, you lucky bastard. You owe me one.'

'Where did you come from?' asked Vic in a relieved tone.

'I was in the neighborhood,' replied Tony British. 'What should I do about the girl?' he asked.

'What girl?' Vic asked.

'They had a sniper in position ready to take you out,' replied Tony British. 'I commandeered her weapon and used it to take out Glass and that other bloke. I have her handcuffed over there.'

Vic went over to have a look at the woman and noticed that it was Elizabeth. He said, 'Look at you all cuffed up just the way you like it, don't you darling?'

She did not speak, so Vic grabbed her towards him and their lips locked in a passionate kiss. She protested a bit, but was quickly subdued by the passion that resonated within her. She still looked stunning even after Tony British had roughed her up and he wished he could have her there and then, but he restrained himself. She stared at him intensely and he pushed her away from his body as he thought about the double cross.

Tony British now joined by the three old men looked at the couple in astonishment.

'I think they are in love,' said McDougal laughing.

'So it seems,' said Nelson and they all laughed.

Vic had pushed her away with so much force that she fell over and was now lying on the ground. He shouted, 'Leave her, she is a cop. She has been working for Glass all along. Using me to satisfy her devilish desire to conquer men, but you failed this time Elizabeth Somerset. You will never have me.'

'She is a what?' asked a surprised Tony, who immediately scanned the area for the quickest escape route. 'That explains the handcuffs. We will have to shoot her,' he suggested in an edgy tone.

'No,' said Vic. 'She will have a lot of explaining to do

and we won't say anything if she doesn't. Come on Tony let us get these bodies on board the ship for these old men are going on a voyage to paradise and these dead men are going on a voyage to the bottom of the sea.'

'Poor old Randy' said JJ. 'I liked the big fella. Are we going to leave him at sea with those two bastards over there?'

'No, I aim to give him a proper burial, for he was my best friend,' replied Vic with glossy eyes.

Vic hugged his father and shook the hands of JJ and McDougal and wished them bon voyage. The three old men waved at the two standing on the docks with tears in their eyes but with strength in their hands for they were off to where they belonged smashing against the waves of the high seas.

'What will you do now Vic?' asked Tony British.

'I could use a drink of Tear Jerker,' replied Vic.

'Well it is your lucky day again Vic. I have some in my car and I still have that lorry with the whisky, so you don't have to bother me about that. I think I should stick with you maybe some of that luck will rub off on me,' said Tony British.

'You thieving bastard!' said Vic.

Both men laughed as they departed the dockyard in McDougal's lorry.

The End